Weddings By the Glass

WEDDINGS by the GLASS

Marc Rubenstein

NEW YORK

NASHVILLE • MELBOURNE • VANCOUVER

Weddings By the Glass

Published in New York, New York, by Morgan James Publishing. Morgan James is a trademark of Morgan James, LLC. www.MorganJamesPublishing.com

The Morgan James Speakers Group can bring authors to your live event. For more information or to book an event visit The Morgan James Speakers Group at www.TheMorganJamesSpeakersGroup.com.

ISBN 9781683505570 paperback
ISBN 9781683505587 eBook
Library of Congress Control Number: 2017906433

Cover Design by:
Rachel Lopez
www.r2cdesign.com

Interior Design by:
Chris Treccani
www.3dogdesign.net

In an effort to support local communities, raise awareness and funds, Morgan James Publishing donates a percentage of all book sales for the life of each book to Habitat for Humanity Peninsula and Greater Williamsburg.

Get involved today! Visit
www.MorganJamesBuilds.com

To Dr. Lee Nordan, an inspiration to all who knew him.

In loving memory of Hilda (Hilly) Cherney, my devoted friend who faithfully accompanied me to hundreds of weddings through the years. Hilly, I'll never forget your greeting, "Tell me something good." It still makes me smile.

In memory of Flory and Felix Van Beek. It was my privilege to be your rabbi at Temple Isaiah of Newport Beach for twenty-five years. You continue to inspire me.

Contents

Acknowledgments

I want to thank all my supporters and friends for participating in this process and agreeing to appear in the book.

First, I would like to thank Ken and Christina, owners of Gershon Bachus Vintners. What a pleasure and privilege to be a part of the kosher-style wine offering. You inspire me, my friends.

Many thanks to Amanda and Ross, whose deeply spiritual wedding I was so blessed and fortunate to officiate.

Thank you to Lindsay Burges, owner of the Hotel Playa Fiesta, where the sunsets and the settings are incredible.

Finally, thank you to Evan Sillings for his many valuable ideas and contributions that enhanced the development and writing of *Weddings By The Glass*.

Introduction

Weddings By The Glass is a novel about love: the love that two people share for each other as they plan and prepare for their wedding, the love of their family and friends and the support they provide, and the love that imbues the wedding ceremony as two people are bound together in marriage

In my over forty years as a rabbi, I have performed more than three thousand weddings, many of them interfaith ceremonies. Approximately 65% of Jewish people marry someone of another faith, yet the vast majority of rabbis still insist that all weddings must conform to Jewish religious tradition, rather than the wishes of the couple. Most engaged couples do not realize or are not aware of the options available to them. Interfaith couples should have the opportunity to have a customized wedding ceremony, whatever their faith, that represents their love for each other, *their spirituality*, and their promises for a bright future together.

That's why I decided to write *Weddings by the Glass* as a fictional story instead of a non-fiction book filled with facts. In this novel I wish to tell a love story that shows, not tells, the heart of the matter: a couple in love who want their wedding to reflect their unique story and fulfill their dream in the most meaningful and spiritual way possible. More than just a party for family and friends, the wedding is the launch of a new life, and having the ceremony reflect that sets the stage for this new beginning.

This story of Hillie and Jay is not only deeply heartfelt and fun, but also educational and informational, with resources boxes, links, and information to use when creating your own customized wedding. In reading *Weddings by the Glass*, the prospective bride can experience through the story the detailed planning of a wedding and the wedding ceremony from start to finish, as opposed to randomly searching through various books and bridal magazines for snippets of inspiration. The story brings the beauty of the actual process to life in a way that brides can relate to and identify with. Share the book with friends or those you know who are planning their wedding.

If you're looking for any assistance in choosing an officiant who will make your dream wedding come true, please send me an email, or join me on my Facebook page and tell me your story. I'd love to hear from you.

Best wishes,
Rabbi Marc Rubenstein
myrabbimarc@gmail.com
WeddingsByTheGlass.com

Chapter 1

The Proposal

Life is a gift that G-d gives you.
What you give back to life, is your gift back to G-d and life.
~ Dr. Lee Nordan

Who on earth gets up this early on a Saturday? Hilary Gordon thought, watching the hot air balloon billowing to life from its place on the stony field. Her boyfriend, Jay Jaworski, had insisted their weekend in Temecula Valley begin with this balloon ride. She would have rather slept in and ordered room service. She yawned and rested her cheek against the crest of his shoulder. He put his arm around her and kissed her hair. His windbreaker felt smooth and comforting.

Half an hour later, their balloon rose above the skyline. Shadowy hilltops formed muted curves against the purple sky, massive stone and stucco buildings scattered here and there. On the south side of Temecula, the land spoke for itself. Gravel driveways wound around and through the hills—little traffic and little fanfare, big heart and gigantic passion.

Though close, the city felt far away.

Like a slow-motion replay, they passed over a winery in the silent dawn above rows of grapevines in rank and file like a marching band at halftime. The sun blinked, then blasted over the hills. The landscape lit up. Suddenly Hillie felt like she was in a fairytale.

In the center of an expansive lawn below, a wrought-iron dome covered a gazebo. On three sides, curtains made of pearl strands moved gently in the breeze. Clusters of pink peonies and white hydrangeas decorated the Greek columns. Long strands of green vines swayed in the breeze. A wide walkway led to a stone building with hanging lanterns on both sides. Wooden folding chairs covered half the lawn.

Hillie pointed and shouted, "A wedding!"

Jay's full lips sort of pulled in as he beamed at her.

With the wind whipping her long dark hair across her face and the whoosh of the blast valve overhead, Hilary had to focus to hear Jay's reply. She turned toward him, then realized he was down on one knee beside her.

"Will you marry me, Hillie?" he asked, holding out an open black box with a sparkling diamond inside.

She gasped. It took her a couple of breaths before she could get out, "Yes!" She leaned over to hug him, laughing deep in her throat.

They had been together for four years and had often talked about marriage, but Jay had caught her completely off guard. She assumed he might surprise her over the holidays, but this was only August.

He stood up to slide the ring on her finger, a large solitaire on a thin band, winking at the morning sun.

He gazed into her eyes, a little anxious. "Do you like it?"

She held the ring to her heart. "I love it, Jay. And I love you!"

He crushed her to him, and the world melted away.

Marrying Jay was everything she could ever wish for. Did anyone deserve to be so deliriously happy?

Already on a successful career path, Hilary led a set design crew working for a large movie producer in Los Angeles. She started out as an intern while working on her second master's degree—cinematography—after completing her first master's in interior design. The staging company immediately hired her upon graduation, and she got her own crew two years later. Most people burned out after a couple of years in that intense profession, but Hillie thrived on the challenging combination of creativity and organization, research and flair.

She first met Jay on a blind double date set up by Hillie's college friend, Sally Wilson. Sally was dating Jay's friend, Brian Taub, at the time.

Both eye surgeons, Brian and Jay were medical school buddies who ended up working in the same ophthalmologic practice in L.A. When Sally met Jay at an office party, she immediately thought of Hillie and set them up.

Sally and Brian had met them at the entrance to Olvera Street in the historic district of L.A. They planned to stroll through the shops and eventually end up with dinner and dancing in town. Sally and Brian couldn't be more different. Similar to Reese Witherspoon, Sally was fair with a sparkling personality while Brian was dark in his appearance and his demeanor. A nice guy, he managed to look downhearted even when he wasn't.

When Sally introduced Jay to Hillie, Jay nodded with a shy smile and shook Hillie's hand. He had a mop of curly dark hair and the biggest brown eyes she had ever seen. Unfortunately, he didn't seem happy to be there.

For the next half hour, she and Jay tagged along with Sally and her guy. Hillie felt a little dismayed. Why didn't he say something?

"Oh, the Avila Adobe!" she blurted out when she saw the sign ahead.

"The oldest residence in Los Angeles," Jay said, looking her full in the face for the first time.

Hillie glanced toward Brian and Sally disappearing in the crowd ahead. "Let's go in!" she said, mischief in her voice.

He grinned as they headed down the narrow alley. "I love this place!" he said when they reached the courtyard. "You can smell the old stone and feel the travelers riding in on their horses." He had a boyish man-face, firm but kind of soft around the edges. Totally cute, now that she thought about it.

"Jedediah Smith stayed here," she finished. "He was the first person from the East to arrive in the area."

"How did you know that?" he demanded.

"History minor. UC Berkeley."

"Me too! But I went to Stanford."

She smirked. "I'll try to forgive you for that. No promises though."

His chin raised as he chuckled.

They never did connect up with Sally and Brian again and ended up having fish tacos at a little shop before finishing the day with a walk on the beach.

And the rest, as they say, is history.

Although not religious himself, Jay—born Jacob Benjamin Jaworski—came from an observant Jewish family. Hillie felt the same about religion, except her family was Catholic. As their relationship deepened, they talked at length about their religious trainings, their respect for their parents' traditions, and their combined desire to make thoughtful choices for themselves instead of simply following tradition.

Hillie's father had no problem with Jay's Jewish heritage. Whatever Hillie wanted, she got, as far as Larry Gordon was concerned. She went to the best schools, received a new car every two years, and he still gave her a generous monthly allowance, though she had told him time and again she didn't need it. He just laughed and told her to save it for a rainy day. Self-sufficient and independent, Hillie remained Daddy's girl, if only to make him happy. After her mother's death fifteen years ago, the two of them hung tight.

Dad often hugged her and whispered, "You look just like your mother, sweetheart. You're about the same age as when we first met, you know." He drew back to look at her, his eyes misty.

"Oh, Dad," she hugged him hard. "I don't want to make you cry."

He shook his head. "It's not you. It's me being an old fool. She would want me to move on, I know. But I can't seem to do it."

That was Dad. He worked on the top floor of a sterile financial planning company, pushing numbers around all day and being professional. Another side came out when he and Hillie were together, and she adored him for it.

Dad liked Jay and admired him for getting so far in his career so quickly. Sometimes they got together for a few rounds of golf without Hillie along. She hated golf and wasn't shy about saying so. Whenever the G-word came up, she'd wave at them and say, "Me and Netflix have a date. I'm researching a set design. Have fun!" They'd grin at each other like two kids cutting class and head for the door.

On the other hand, Jay's mother had serious objections to Jay's choice of a girlfriend, and she let Jay know that at every possible opportunity, especially family dinners.

Olivia Jaworski's bird-like hands worried with the cloth napkin on her lap. Peach-colored linen covered their dinner table, set with the gold-rimmed everyday china and crystal goblets filled with Moscato wine.

"She's a nice girl, Jacob," Olivia said, "but there are a lot of nice Jewish girls out there, like… What was her name you dated? Candy…?"

"Candy Cohen," Jay said. He felt his mouth twisting and forced a calm expression. "That was in tenth grade."

"That's right. Candy Cohen. Good Jewish family and nice girl. Why not her?"

Jay knew better than to answer his mother. One word from him, and she would start crying. That was the worst. He stared at his half-eaten baked potato and waited. His father would intervene. That's the way things worked at their house. At least Hillie wasn't present to hear this.

"Leave the boy alone," Max said, as though on cue. "He's a grown man, thirty-two years old. He's going to date who he wants to date." He took a bite of sirloin.

"Ach…" Disgusted, she dropped her napkin to the tablecloth and got up to fetch something from the kitchen. Thin and small boned, Olivia seemed to grow smaller and more intense every year.

Max winked at Jay. Max Jaworski had been a pharmaceutical sales rep for more than thirty years. Weighing in at less than a hundred and fifty pounds, he had wiry strength that seemed to pump out internal energy.

"What do you get when a non-practicing Jew crosses with a non-practicing Catholic?" Max asked, while chewing his steak.

"What?" Eyebrows raised, Jay reached for his wine glass.

Max picked up his own wine glass. "I don't know, but somebody's gonna feel guilty." He held out his glass to clink, raised it to his son, and then drank.

Jay and Hillie's Temecula engagement weekend was a magic carpet ride that lasted all the way to their soulful good-bye kiss at the door of Hillie's third floor walkup.

What a sweet, sweet guy, Hillie thought as she closed the door behind her. *Could her life be more perfect?*

Flicking on lights, she dropped her luggage and pulled out her cellphone. "Hi, Dad," she said when he picked up. "I just got back from Temecula." On the other end, Larry Gordon's deep chuckle filled her heart and made her smile.

"Tell me something good!" he said, a greeting started by her mother that had become a family tradition.

The tone of his voice made Hillie gasp. "You know!"

"Jay told me six weeks ago. I promised him I'd keep the secret."

"I wish Mom could meet Jay," she said. "Mom would love him."

"Yes she would, sweetheart." He paused for a long moment. "I'm glad you're happy. That means everything. You'll call me if you need anything…"

She nodded. "Thanks, Dad. I love you."

"…I love you too, baby."

Sinking into the soft chair near the door, she drew in a long breath and let the feeling of deep loss waft through her. She still cried over her mother at times. This was one of those times.

Deeply spiritual, Hillie had learned that sitting with her emotions for a few moments would let them process through her and evaporate, so she wouldn't get stuck in grief and loss for the rest of the night. This was a time for celebration, not crying. Mom wouldn't have wanted that either. Best to let it out now.

As the moment passed, Hillie whispered, "I'll find a way to take you with me, Mom. You're going to be there for the whole thing." Sinking her chin to her chest, she hugged herself and gently rocked.

Finally, Hillie wiped her face. Rolling her suitcase into the only bedroom of her small apartment, she felt tired. All the emotions of the weekend were taking their toll. She wanted a shower and a good night's sleep.

But first…

She reached up to the top shelf of her closet and pulled out a presentation folder with a snap closure. Slipping out of her sandals, she spilled the contents onto her white bedspread.

Working in the interior design industry, Hillie didn't have the time or energy to devote to her own space, so most everything in her apartment was white from the walls to the furniture, to the lamps and fixtures. Even the framed art consisted of black-and-white photos, some personal and some purchased. Living in a blank environment seemed more restful to her.

She sat on the bed and sifted through the pile of papers beside her. Her fingers automatically went to a cut-out of a wedding dress about twelve inches tall. Scuffed with a crease on one corner, it had a massive lace skirt and a tiny strapless bodice, an old-fashioned style that was coming back, oddly enough.

From the time she was five years old, Hillie and her mother had played the Wedding Game. It had started with a box of paper dolls Hillie had found at the bottom of the toy box at her grandmother's house. The box was bent and scarred. One corner of the lid had split open. On the top, a beautiful girl with long dark hair wore an enormous wedding gown.

"What's this?" young Hillie had asked, bringing the box to her mother who was sitting in Grandma's living room. Tall and slim, Mom had her long wavy hair pulled back into a wide barrette.

"My paper dolls!" Mom had cried out, smiling at Grandma Margaret. "I haven't seen these in years!"

Grandma sipped from her china cup. "I couldn't bear to throw that box away, Melissa. Remember how you used to play with them at the kitchen table?"

"Hours and hours on rainy days," Mom said. She took the box on her lap and opened the lid. "See?" she told Hillie. "You take the cardboard girl and push her feet into this stand, so she'll stand up."

She had set the figure on the coffee table in front of her and reached into the box. "Here's the wedding gown." She fastened the wedding dress onto the standing girl by folding the paper tabs over her cardboard shoulders.

Here was that same paper dress now. She smoothed the crease and felt her grandmother's soft smile. Hillie propped the dress against the pillow sham. The cardboard doll figure was long gone.

Sorting the images of cakes from the photos of bouquets and bridesmaids gowns, Hillie felt a brief urge to cry again, but it quickly passed. She would be thirty years old next May, but deep inside her that five-year-old girl still clung to the wish for a magical day she'd remember for the rest of her life.

She reached down to the bottom drawer of her bedside stand and found her parents' wedding album. She'd seen the pictures thousands of times, but now each detail took on new meaning. Her mother's stiff tulle veil, the decorations—Hillie wanted to incorporate some of these into her own wedding as a private memorial to her sweet mother.

Closing the wedding album, she laid it beside the paper mound beside her. She glanced at the clock. It was past midnight.

Never mind. She had to know now or she wouldn't sleep anyway.

Fetching the stepstool from the kitchen, she reached to the third shelf at the top of her closet and pulled out a long box. Two other boxes came with it and burst open on the floor. She ignored them.

With great reverence, she lifted her mother's wedding dress, carefully wrapped all these years. Crumpled and flattened, it was still in good shape. No yellowing. No tearing or dry rotting.

A simple A-line design with a short train, the top had two lace straps over the shoulders. It had a silk underskirt and filmy organza overskirt with hand-sewn beading and embellishments. So classic and breathtakingly beautiful.

Could she get into it? As the gown fell down around her, the smell of the fabric filled her senses. Her mother's scent. Hillie lost her breath for a moment.

The dress buttoned up the back so she couldn't fasten it herself, but the top seemed a bit loose and the waist would fit. She could have it altered. Standing before the mirrored doors on her closet, she rubbed the smooth skirt. For a flickering moment, she saw her mother gazing back at her in the glass, almost an exact replica of her parents' wedding picture.

This was the answer. She would have the wedding she once pictured with her mother when she was five years old. Mom would be with her when she wore this dress.

Chapter 2

The Officiant

Tell me something good.
~ Hilda Cherney

H er staging crew was finishing up a set and that meant a million details to take care of throughout the next few weeks. Finding time to interview rabbis added more stress to her already stressful life.

Hillie wanted an interfaith wedding that brought in both Jewish and Christian traditions with a feeling of fun and celebration. She wanted it to focus on their story. The first step: finding a rabbi to officiate the ceremony. She searched out the rabbis in the area and started making calls to set up appointments. Most of them wanted to meet her via Skype, so she tried to schedule those appointments on her lunch break. She felt frustrated at how detached these meetings felt, talking to a stranger while holding up her phone—the set crew laughing and talking all around her.

This was the most sacred occasion of her life, and she was trying to use such sketchy contact to make a vital decision. It wasn't working for her.

She stopped scheduling Skype calls. If the rabbi wouldn't see her in person, she crossed them off her list.

Late on a Sunday afternoon in September, Jay and Hillie left a rabbi's office—their third appointment that afternoon—and headed to Giorgio's to enjoy the best Greek pastitsio in town. They were eager to sit down together in a quiet, comfortable space and compare their impressions.

A quiet place with hand-painted murals and a dark wooden bar off to one side, Giorgio's was their choice about twice a month. The owner's son, Angelo, seated them at their favorite booth and took their order. No need for a menu here.

A moment later, he returned with their drinks and a basket of warm crusty bread.

When they were alone, Hillie opened her notebook—a bound journal with a brown leather cover. "What did you think of the first one… Rabbi Goldman?

Jay cocked his head to one side. "Eh…"

She tucked a dark curl behind her ear and waited, pen in hand. "Is that a yes or a no?"

Dipping a chunk of torn bread into a small dish of oil, he said, "He didn't impress me one way or the other. Neither did the third one we talked to. Once they found out you're not Jewish, they both pretty much wrote us off." He popped the bread into his mouth.

She crossed out two names.

"So Number 2. Rabbi…" She looked closer. "…Appelbaum. He is younger and seems to have more energy."

"But he's also very set in the traditions," Jay said, shaking his head. "He told you it's your duty to encourage me to keep my

Jewishness. If we have him officiate, we'll have a Jewish wedding, strictly by the book. Is that what you want?"

"I want the service to mean something for our future, sort of like a launch to our life together." She drew in a long breath. "Is that too much to ask?"

Jay reached out to cover her hand. "You're going to have exactly that, Hillie. We'll find the right rabbi."

"I hope so. Today makes ten appointments so far, and no good possibility yet. How many rabbis are there in Orange County?"

"Are you sure you want to have the wedding in Orange County?" he asked.

"That's a good point. I'm not sure where to have the wedding— the beach is a nice choice, or a park, or a winery. More decisions!"

"All in good time." Jay leaned closer. "Let's stop talking for a while, okay? I want to sit here and stare into your gorgeous green eyes."

She tilted her head and smiled. He lifted her hand and brought it to his lips.

Over the next week, the wedding constantly hovered in the back of Hillie's mind. She was a planner and not having the basic elements to get started with actual wedding preparation was making her crazy.

On Monday after work, Hillie drove to her hot yoga class. She did hot yoga three times a week as part of her secret weapon against burnout. Sweating out the toxins and stretching her tense muscles kept her in the game. Except for vacation travel, she hadn't missed a class in three years.

Yoga helped, for sure. So did talking with her friend, Amanda Weinstein, who owned the studio.

On her way out, Hillie paused next to Amanda's open office door and knocked on the door frame. "Got a minute?" she asked.

The office barely had room for a tall filing cabinet and a desk with one folding chair facing it. Almost covering the back wall, a giant parchment poster said *Namaste* in Sanskrit and English.

Typing furiously on her computer keyboard, Amanda looked up. "Sure, honey. What's up?" She wore all black and had her long blond hair in a high ponytail.

"I won't keep you long," Hillie said, plopping into the chair and pressing a towel to her streaming face. She let her tote bag slip to the floor.

Amanda slid her desk chair sideways, away from the computer in the corner. Slim and taut with a healthy glow, Amanda could have been on the cover of a wellness magazine, even without makeup. "Everything okay?" she asked.

"Jay and I are great," Hillie said, "but I've run into a roadblock on the wedding plans. I can't find a rabbi who will do the ceremony the way I want it—with some Jewish elements and then some things that Jay and I want that aren't necessarily Jewish."

"I get it." Amanda nodded. "Are you planning to convert?"

"You mean become Jewish?" Hillie shook her head. "We talked about it. But I'm not religious, and neither is Jay. It would feel weird to join a religion when I have no desire to really embrace the traditions." She sighed. "It's not authentic."

"Definitely not the right reason for a decision like that," Amanda said. "And good for you for keeping it real."

"It's something we've given some serious thought to." Hillie shared her concerns about her distant relationship with Jay's mother. "Can you imagine making a false promise like that and then not following through? Things would only get worse."

"Hillie, I have just the rabbi for you," Amanda said. "His name is Rabbi Samuel Glassman. He's so kind and totally dedicated to creating a unique wedding for each couple—no matter what kind of religious collage they're piecing together via matrimony." She smiled. "Actually, he married Ross and me, so I can vouch for how awesome he is."

"Do you have his contact information?" Hillie pulled her cellphone from her tote bag.

Amanda moved to her computer and tapped the keys. She wrote on a yellow sticky note and handed it to Hillie. "Here you go. I wrote down his website and his number. Please tell him I sent you and that I said hello. You're going to love him, Hillie."

"You are an angel!" Hillie jumped up to hug Amanda, an awkward move since Amanda was still sitting behind the desk. "I won't keep you longer," she said, heading for the door. "Thank you!" She was already dialing.

On Monday evenings Jay met with his Fantasy Football league after work, so Hillie waited until Tuesday evening to fill him in on Rabbi Glassman.

Over chicken dinner at her place, she finished with, "Last night I left voicemail asking for an appointment. His website looks good." She glanced at her phone on the table. "I hope you don't mind. My phone is still on, in case he calls." They usually turned off their phones at mealtimes.

Jay dug into his macaroni and cheese. "If he calls that fast, it will be a record."

At that moment, the phone vibrated and chirped.

She laughed. "It's him!" She picked up. "Hilary speaking." She paused, then said, "I'm putting you on speakerphone."

"This is Rabbi Sam Glassman returning your call," he said, his voice mellow. "Some people call me Marrying Sam." He said it with a chuckle in his voice. "I'm honored to meet you, Hilary."

Hillie placed the phone on the table corner between Jay and her. "My fiancé Jay's here with me," she said.

"Wonderful to meet you both," he said. "How can I help you?"

She told of her frustrating search for a wedding officiant, ending with Amanda's glowing recommendation.

"Amanda had a wonderful wedding," Rabbi Sam said. "They were at Rancho Las Cruces in Baja California. It was a historic moment, so powerful and meaningful."

"We'd like to meet with you to talk with possibly officiating our wedding," Hillie said.

"Of course. I always like to talk with both people at our first meeting," he said. "Do you have your calendars? We can set something up now." They scheduled a meeting for the following Sunday afternoon at an outdoor cafe.

Before leaving the call, Rabbi Sam promised to send them both an email with information they'd need in order to prepare for their meeting.

Switching off her phone, Hillie beamed. "I think we're finally on the right track," she said. "This one feels different, don't you think?"

Jay grinned. "I hope so," he said, sipping wine. "You know I'd be happy with a quick trip to Vegas."

"Vegas, huh?" She quirked in the corner of her mouth then reached over to kiss him.

He gazed into her eyes. "I want you to be happy. You know that, right?"

"I am happy. That's why we're here." She kissed him again. "Eat your dinner, Jock." Her takeoff on *Jacob*. "I want to see what the rabbi emails us."

He groaned. "You mean there's homework after dinner?"

She playfully pushed his shoulder. "You're such a kid!"

By the time they finished dinner, Rabbi Sam had sent them the promised email with his web site and a document called "50 Things

Rabbi Sam Does at a Wedding Service That Other Rabbis Might Not Do."

The following Sunday, Rabbi Sam met Jay and Hillie at Rosa's Cantina in Old Town Temecula. The restaurant had an adobe arch leading to an outdoor dining area with rainbow-striped umbrellas over each table. Wearing a dark suit jacket with an open collar, Rabbi Sam sat near the doorway when they arrived. Hillie recognized him from his website. He had a mound of thick hair falling over his forehead and twinkling blue eyes behind his Clark Kent glasses.

He stood when he caught sight of them. "Hilary and Jay?" he asked. His voice sounded rich with a smile in it.

Hillie nodded, shaking hands. "My friends call me Hillie," she said. "Just think of the character in *Beaches*, and you've got it."

"I've got it!" He beamed.

Jay shook hands with the rabbi. "Jacob Jaworski. Thank you for meeting us."

As they found their seats, Rabbi Sam said, "Amanda called me after you did. She was so excited she couldn't wait." He laughed. "A lovely girl. Beautiful inside and out."

Hillie pulled her leather journal from her purse. "Amanda owns the yoga studio I go to. You are right. She is a lovely person."

The server appeared and took their coffee orders.

"Tell me your story," Rabbi Sam said. "How did you meet?" He took a small notebook from his jacket pocket and opened to a fresh page.

Hillie told him about their blind date, including their walk through Avila Adobe and ending up on the beach. "He called me the next day to set up another date, and we've been together ever since," she said, sharing a smile with Jay.

"And that was four years ago?" he asked, making notes.

"He proposed last month when we were at a weekend right here in Temecula."

He looked up. "What a beautiful place to get engaged! Tell me how you pulled that off, Jay."

"She wasn't expecting it," he said, pulling in his lower lip. "I totally surprised her."

"He practically forced me to go up in a hot air balloon," Hillie chimed in. "I'm sorry to say I was a little grumpy getting up so early."

"A little!" Jay countered.

She pushed his arm.

She turned to Rabbi Sam. "We hovering over a winery with a wedding set up in the yard right under us. It was pretty amazing."

"Let's see the ring," Rabbi Sam said.

She held it out.

"Not bad, Mr. Jaworski," he said, nodding. "Not bad at all."

"What do you like most about weddings?" Rabbi Sam asked.

Jay blurted out. "Leaving the reception." He glanced at Hillie.

"He keeps saying he'd rather go to Vegas," Hillie said.

"It's a lot," Rabbi Sam agreed. "A lot of details. A lot of family stuff comes up. A lot of stress."

"I want Hillie to be happy," Jay told him. "That's my main concern. We haven't started with the actual wedding prep yet, and she's already getting stressed out. This should be a happy time for us. I don't like seeing her frustrated and under pressure."

"We can help relieve some of that stress," Rabbi Sam told them. "I've been doing this for more than forty years, so I have a lot of resources and contacts to help smooth the way for you. I do every wedding as if it were my own and the only wedding I ever did."

He nodded toward a blue folder on the table beside him. "Here are some things I put together for you to look at later, and I'll also email you some links to look at."

Focusing on Jay, he went on, "Tell me about your family, Jay. What's their attitude toward your upcoming wedding to a non-Jewish girl?"

Jay hesitated, his expression tense.

"It's okay, sweetheart," Hillie said. "We have to put everything on the table."

He put his arm around Hillie. "My father is great. He loves Hillie, and he's happy I found someone so wonderful."

"Your mother?" Rabbi Sam prompted.

"She's on a loop, and she never stops playing," he said. "I'm starting to dread going to family dinners."

"We'll talk about this more in our pre-wedding counseling—as my client you get an unlimited number of sessions with me before the wedding—but what I want to impress on you now is that we can take some steps to help your mother feel a little better. This kind of family tension is something I deal with all the time… almost weekly."

Jay's shoulders relaxed. "If you could help us get through the wedding with everyone still speaking to us…" He exhaled and his cheeks puffed out.

Rabbi Sam nodded. "I can't promise 100% success, but we can use some strategies that might help." He adjusted his glasses. "As far as the ceremony itself, my ceremonies usually go 22½ minutes long."

Hillie burst out laughing. "Not twenty-three minutes?" she asked.

He chuckled. "Actually from twenty-two minutes to thirty minutes, depending on what you want. I sent you my list of fifty things I do differently…"

"…Yes, I went through that," Hillie said. "Coming early, staying for the reception, and even checking on the flower girl and ring bearer for a potty break." She glanced at Jay. "It was impressive."

"Forty years' worth of experience. But most important of all is my promise to you that I will do everything in my power to help you have the wedding of your dreams." He leaned forward to look into their eyes. "What people will remember about the wedding is what I say about you and what you say to each other. That's what I'd like you to focus on."

He paused and drew a long breath. "Hillie, tell me your vision for your wedding. What do you have in mind?"

"I want to honor Jay's family. They're observant, even though he's not. I want to make the wedding respectful to them," she said, "but I also want to honor my mother and her dreams for my wedding."

"That's what you want for everyone else," he told her. "What do you want yourself?"

She paused and looked at Jay. "I want something meaningful that will be a wonderful memory for the rest of our lives. I want a beautiful wedding to launch our beautiful marriage."

"And so you shall," Rabbi Sam promised. "What I love to do is help you create a ceremony that does two things: It honors the heritage of both people, and it has meaning for your future together. It will be Your Unique Special Day."

Hillie leaned into Jay. He still had his arm around her.

"Anything else?" Rabbi Sam asked.

"My mother passed away when I was fifteen." She told him about her wedding folder and the Wedding Game she used to play with her mother, where they would pretend to plan Hillie's wedding using magazine cuttings and catalog pictures.

"I have my mother's gown and her wedding album. My plan is to have the dress altered and use some of the elements from my parents' wedding as a tribute to her." She touched her necklace.

Rabbi Sam leaned forward for a closer look. "That's beautiful, Hillie."

"It's a blue moonstone. My mom gave this to me when I turned thirteen."

Jay added, "She was born on the rare blue moon in May of '88."

Rabbi Sam nodded. "And you're going to have a rare wedding, too, Hillie. Just as rare and unique as you are." He made a note in his notebook. "What else do you have in mind for the wedding?"

"I'm thinking a destination wedding," she said. "The beach, a beautiful hotel or resort, possibly a winery… I don't really know yet."

"Tell you what…" He considered for a moment. "Why don't you come with me as my guests to a couple of weddings? Then you can see how I work and also check out some locations."

"That would be over-the-top amazing," Hillie said. Her heartbeat picked up speed.

"I'll send you some places and dates, and we'll see what works." He opened the blue folder on the table. "In the meantime, I'd like to recommend that you connect with InterfaithFamily. They help couples who have a Jewish spouse and a non-Jewish spouse." He pulled a flyer from the folder. "Here are their services and…" pointing at the back, "their website."

He looked from Jay to Hillie. "This is your wedding day, the biggest day of your life up to now. It would be my privilege to help you make it a wonderful success for everyone." He smiled. "There are three things you have to do for me, though."

Both of them waited, watching him. Hillie held her pen.

"I want you to practice kissing, drinking wine, and holding hands."

They all laughed.

Jay kissed Hillie's temple. She sat so close to him that her wavy hair brushed his cheek. "Would you like to think it over?" he asked, looking at her.

She shook her head. "After what I've seen, there's nothing else to talk about." She reached for her purse. "Can I write you a check, Rabbi Sam?"

InterfaithFamily: Supporting Interfaith Families Supporting Jewish Life

Originally an online magazine launched in 1998, *InterfaithFamily* empowers people in interfaith relationships—individuals, couples, families and their children—to engage in Jewish life and make Jewish choices. It also encourages Jewish communities to welcome them.

InterfaithFamily is the leading producer of Jewish resources and content, either online or in print, designed for people in interfaith relationships. They deliver helpful, non-judgmental information and a warm welcome that can be accessed privately, at any time convenient to the user. They offer downloadable Resource Guides to Jewish holidays and life-cycle ceremonies, along with "The Guide to Jewish Interfaith Family Life: An InterfaithFamily.com Handbook."

Their Jewish Clergy Officiation Referral Service is a free, high-quality service that helps over 2,000 interfaith couples a year find a rabbi or cantor to officiate or co-officiate at their weddings and other life-cycle events.

Their Community Page centralizes all local information and encourages couples to talk about religion in their lives, and create personal relationships that lead to more Jewish engagement.

Visit www.InterfaithFamily.com for more information.

Chapter 3

Rancho Las Cruces

May you cry in each other's tears
and laugh in each other's smile.
~ Rabbi Marc Rubenstein

The next Destination Wedding on Rabbi Sam's calendar was at Rancho Las Cruces in Baja California, a luxurious resort overlooking the Sea of Cortés on the eastern side of the Baja Peninsula. Since the location was quite a distance from L.A., Hillie and Jay decided to cash in a couple of personal days at work and make a four-day weekend of it. They needed a break and this would be the perfect time to enjoy the resort.

The shuttle bus arrived at Rancho Las Cruces and stopped outside a locked gate. The driver got out to punch in a code and swing the gates wide. After they entered the resort, they continued driving another ten minutes.

Stepping out of the bus felt like stepping into a dream. On one side rose the Santa Cruz Mountains and on the other side the peaceful Sea of Cortés sparkled in the sun. The constant urgency of Los Angeles slid off them as quickly and easily as a silk scarf caught by the breeze. When they reached their cabaña, the steward brought in their luggage and gave them a short tour. Hillie didn't hear a word he said. She stood at the bank of wide windows, lost in the sea vista just outside. *This is what they would wake up to every morning?*

Their suite had a sitting area with a fireplace. Ornate urns and *objets d'art* filled lighted cut-outs sunk into the thick cream-colored walls. A covered tray waited on the coffee table along with a bottle of wine on ice. Their lunch.

 She slipped off her shoes, and the cool tile floor drained the tension of travel from her body. She stooped down to touch the ceramic squares and had a sudden urge to lie down and press her cheek on them like she did when she was five years old. She smiled. She hadn't thought of that in years.

Each room had an air conditioner but with the ocean breeze, they didn't need it. The wind felt so good. Meals came with the room, also a daily maid and laundry service—nothing to do and no place to go for four whole days.

"I'm going to shower," she told Jay, twisting up her dark hair and fastening it with a giant clip. "If I can get an hour nap, I'll be good to go."

He pulled the linen cloth off the food tray. "I hope you don't mind if I eat something while you're in there. I'm starving." He pulled plastic wrap off a bowl of fruit salad.

"No rules while we're here, my love," she called over her shoulder. "I'm in heaven right now. Don't wake me up!"

They played in the sea, ate way too much food, and drank way too much wine for the next forty-eight hours. With an effort, they came back to reality long enough to dress for the wedding—reluctantly reminding themselves this was the reason they were at Rancho Las Cruces in the first place.

The wedding took place at 3:00. A little before 1:00, Hillie and Jay visited the reception hall to have a look before the room filled with guests.

The large room had chairs along the walls but the center of the area was wide open. "For dancing," Jay told her. At the front of the room a small table held several items including two large wine glasses, a golden goblet, and a silver ice bucket standing ready. Near the table two chairs had white slipcovers on them. The back of one said, Mr. Right. The other said, Mrs. Always Right.

"What are those for?" Hillie asked.

"The bride and groom sit on them, and the crowd raises them up until the wedding couple sits above the crowd."

"I'm not sure I want to do that one," she said, doubtfully.

Along one side of the room, six buffet tables held sterno burners ready to keep chafing dishes warm. On the other side, a team assembled the wedding cake. Sounds of clanging pans and conversation wafted from the kitchen along with delicious aromas.

"That smells like enchiladas," Hillie said. "Let's get out of here before I start asking them for samples."

The ceremony would take place in an open courtyard with the resort's signature three stone crosses above them. Half a mile away, a wedding chapel stood ready in case the weather decided to defy the local forecast.

Hillie and Jay arrived at the site of the wedding more than an hour early. Rabbi Sam was already on duty, beaming with goodwill and watching for details—from repositioning a chair that got knocked askew to chatting with early arrivals. All of the guests were staying at the resort, so more than thirty people were already here and more arriving by the minute. Classical music played in the background.

Observing Rabbi Sam, Hillie could tell he was in his element. This is what he lived for.

When he spotted them, Rabbi Sam ambled over. He wore a dark gray suit, a tallit folded over his arm. His thick hair riffled in the strong breeze. "Welcome! Are you enjoying the resort?" He chuckled. "I've been here since yesterday and haven't seen you once."

Jay grinned. "We've been incognito." He shook the rabbi's hand.

Hillie shook his hand as well. "Great to see you, Rabbi Sam," she said. "Tell me something good." A dimple appeared in her left cheek.

"What a beautiful day!" he said, turning to scan sun-bleached rocks lining the shore.

"Spectacular!" Hillie said. "I traveled to Europe and Asia with my dad quite a bit, and this is the best I've ever seen. Breathtaking."

Rabbi Sam beamed. "It's one of my favorites, that's for sure. This is star country. Desi Arnaz, Jr. lives next door. His father also lived here. Back in the day, Bing Crosby did, too." He nodded toward a staff member walking across the compound. "You can feel safe here. Their staff is like family. Most of them are children and grandchildren of the original workers."

He gestured toward the wedding site. "As I told you, today we have Jocelyn, a Jewish bride, and Steve, an Anglican groom. This event is going to have some traditional Christian elements along with Jewish, so I'm co-officiating with a priest. When the couple wants to invoke the more traditional Christian elements, that's how it usually works."

Hillie's eyes stayed on the scene before them, drinking in everything—the canopy, the covered table. "I already see some things I don't recognize," she said, holding her leather journal and a pen.

"I'll fill you in," Jay told her.

Rabbi Sam went on, "We had an issue with the food. A few of Jocelyn's family keep kosher, so she made arrangements for a kosher caterer from La Paz to bring in a few kosher meals for them. The rest of the food isn't kosher." He shrugged. "In situations like this, the wedding couple has to get creative to try to keep the peace." He looked at Jay. "You might have to as well, so this is a heads up for you."

Jay's expression didn't change, but Hillie felt his tension.

"I'd best get back to the job," Rabbi Sam said. "Let's meet up for dinner later, okay? That way we can discuss what you liked from today's event. I want to touch base with you before I fly out in the morning." Hillie and Jay were staying until Tuesday. One more day in heaven.

Rabbi Sam stepped away, then turned back. "This is Jocelyn's dream wedding. She's chosen to hold with some traditions and modify others. Nothing is set in stone." He hurried away.

"The canopy is called the *Chuppah*," Jay told her. "It creates a sacred space to have the ceremony. Once the couple goes under the Chuppah, they have a direct connection to the divine." The Chuppah before them was brilliant white with a blue Star of David in the center of the top. Flowers and ribbons decorated the wooden poles.

"It's beautiful," Hillie said. "Is that something you want in our wedding?"

"There are basically two traditions considered essential to Jewish weddings—the Chuppah and Breaking the Glass," he told her. "My family would feel slighted without them." He sounded apologetic.

"It's okay, sweetheart. That's what I need to know. So, we're going to have the Chuppah and Breaking the Glass." She made a note in her journal. When she finished, she asked, "What's on the table?"

He shook his head. "I have no idea. We'll have to wait until they uncover it."

"What? You left your x-ray vision glasses at home? And you're an eye doctor." She pushed his arm. "What were you thinking?"

He put his arm around her and kissed her cheek. "I love it when you sweet talk me like that."

They found seats at the end of the last row, keeping a low profile.

The wedding began at fifteen past three when Rabbi Sam led Steve and six groomsmen to form a line to the right of the Chuppah. Steve wore a white military uniform with a row of medals on his chest.

The music paused, then came back on with more intensity. Hillie didn't recognize the song. She wrote a note to Jay in her journal and showed it to him.

"That's called 'Tumbalalaika'," Jay said. "It's very old."

"It's beautiful." She handed him the journal to write the title down.

Six bridesmaids in pale mauve gowns streamed in, followed by the ring bearer who couldn't have been more than three years old. Dressed in a tux and carrying a white pillow, the little guy yelled, "Grandpa!" and headed straight for a bald portly man sitting on the end of the second aisle. His grandfather spoke gently to the child and guided him toward the front where the second bridesmaid reached for the boy and held his hand.

Jocelyn appeared next. She had long blond hair swept into an up-do with soft ringlets springing free here and there, topped by a sparkling tiara with a filmy veil floating down behind her. Her satin gown had a wide skirt that swished as she moved.

Jocelyn held her father's arm on her right and her mother's arm on her left. They slowly paced down the aisle and paused about six feet from Steve.

"Who gives this woman…?" Rabbi Sam asked.

"We do." Both parents hugged Jocelyn and found their seats in the second row.

Steve stepped forward and looked deeply into Jocelyn's eyes, taking his time. They seemed to be whispering something to each other. Finally, he pulled the top layer of her filmy veil forward to cover her face. Taking her hand, they entered the Chuppah together.

"That's called the Bedeken," Jay said. "He's making sure she's the one for him and covering her."

Hillie looked doubtful. She glanced at the wedding couple and back to Jay.

"Don't worry. That's definitely not required," he whispered in her ear.

She arched her eyebrow at him, and he silently snickered.

Several people stepped forward holding slips of paper. They stepped under the Chuppah and each spoke into the microphone wishing the happy couple joy and abundance.

"That's the Seven Blessings," Jay said.

Nodding, she wrote it down. "I like it."

Rabbi Sam said, "If we add up the frequent flier miles that were accumulated here today, it would not equal the amount of love Jocelyn and Steve have for each other and for you in their hearts." He told the story of how Jocelyn met Steve and how they fell in love.

Then the priest stepped to the front and talked about marriage and how it's a picture of Christ and the church, ending with a long prayer for their marriage.

After the priest led them through the *I Do's* and the rings, Rabbi Sam took the cloth off the table.

Jay said, "That's the Ketubah. The marriage contract."

The document lay flat on the table, so Hillie couldn't see it. She made a note to google it.

Jocelyn and Steve took turns signing the Ketubah, followed by two witnesses and Rabbi Sam. Afterward, Rabbi Sam read the document aloud.

The wedding ended with more Hebrew and another cup of wine. At that point, Steve lifted the veil from Jocelyn's face.

Rabbi Sam placed a folded white cloth on the ground. Steve smashed it with his heel for a loud POP. Everyone cheered, "*Mazel Tov!*" and Steve enfolded Jocelyn into a kiss. The crowd grew noisier with waving arms and shouts.

Jay laughed aloud.

Hillie glanced around, overwhelmed by the chaos and the noise. She was ready to go. Tugging Jay's arm, she got his attention. They made their escape, leaving the area toward the back so as not to be noticed.

"What did you think?" Jay asked when they reached the sidewalk along the sea.

She was panting from the run. "It was loud!"

He burst out laughing. "Jewish weddings are loud. This one was pretty tame, actually." He glanced at her. "You want to peek in at the reception?"

"Maybe we can check in after a couple of hours. I think I've had enough for now… unless you want to..."

"Not me! I'd rather play on the beach for an hour."

"Let's do that!" She dropped her journal into her purse and stretched her back. "Let's open that bottle of wine in the chiller first, okay?"

"Now you're talking!" He was already ahead of her. "Race you to the room!"

Rancho Las Cruces

Discovered on May 3rd, 1535, the Spanish conquistador Hernán Cortés placed three crosses on the land he baptized as Santa Cruz. Later, it became known as Las Cruces. Stone replicas of these crosses still remain at Rancho Las Cruces.

Standing where Cortés once stood more than 400 years earlier, Abelardo L. Rodriguez Montijo took in the enchantment of ten thousand acres with more than seven miles of private sea coast and dreamed of an elite getaway for city dwellers. In 1948 Montijo and his beautiful bride, Lucille Bremer decided to turn Las Cruces into a small luxury resort.

This was the birth of tourism in the Mexican state of Baja California Sur. The success of Las Cruces prompted Abelardo (Rod) to build other world class resorts in Baja. Hotel Palmilla which opened in 1957 is still thought of as the shining star of Los Cabos (now the One and Only Palmilla) as well as Hotel Hacienda in Cabo San Lucas.

Las Cruces, however, was the place Abelardo and his family always called home. Here he built his own home as well as homes for his dear friends and partners Robert Fisher, Desi Arnaz, Bing Crosby, Charles Jones and Roger Bacon. Casa Fisher is now called Hacienda Santa Cruz. These resorts became famous and many celebrities visited here, including princes, presidents, dignitaries and stars. Rancho Las Cruces offers discriminating guests the same natural beauty, tranquility and charm today.

For more information, visit www.RanchoLasCruces. com

Jewish Wedding Traditions

1. Bedeken: By gazing into his bride's eyes, the groom verifies he's marrying the bride of his choice, then he places the veil over his bride's face.
2. Breaking the Glass: Signals that the wedding ceremony is over; the breaking of the glass signifies the permanence of the commitment the couple just made.
3. Chuppah: Wedding tent forming a sacred space for the wedding ceremony, said to create a direct connection to the divine.
4. Hagafen: Hebrew blessing over the wine.
5. Ketubah: Marriage contract signed by the bride and groom, two witnesses, and the officiant. This is often written in beautiful calligraphy with an ornate border and frame to be hung in a prominent place in the home.
6. Seven Blessings: Seven guests step under the Chuppah to read seven good wishes to the wedding couple.
7. Seven Circles around the Groom: The bride walks around the groom seven times to protect him from evil (can also be three times).

Chapter 4

Gershon Bachus Vintners

As you give each other your hand to hold,
may you give each other your heart to keep.
~ Rabbi Marc Rubenstein

Their trip to Rancho Las Cruces left Hillie and Jay feeling dreamy, a much needed break from the strain of the past two months with their hectic schedules and trying to get their wedding off the ground. They landed at LAX airport, and switched on their cell phones.

"I almost hate to do this," Hillie said. Immediately her phone set off in a series of chirps.

Ten messages from her assistant about a disaster on the set— the wrong furniture had arrived and the right furniture would not be available until after shooting began. She spent the drive home on the phone.

"I'll call you back, Becca," Hillie promised. "I've got to say good-bye to Jay." Clicking off the phone without waiting for a response, she said, "Welcome to the real world!"

"I can't wait to call in for my office messages," Jay said. "It's not going to be pretty."

Hillie leaned over for a kiss. "Tell you what," she said. "How about if both of us research some places online and make a list of venues to visit? I don't see how I'll have time to do it all myself at this rate."

"You've got it," he said, opening his car door. "I'll sit down for a while tonight and shoot you an email with some suggestions. Tomorrow morning, my office takes over everything. I have four surgeries stacked up because of the time away."

They spent the next two weekends visiting locations: two popular beachfront venues, three hotels, and a full day spend in Napa Valley talking to wedding coordinators at various wineries.

Jay mentioned Las Vegas more and more, especially at his office Fantasy Football meetings.

Jay practiced at the Jules Stein Eye Institute at UCLA. While in medical school at Stanford, he had heard the legendary ophthalmologist Lee Nordan speak about the importance of being the best doctor in your field, nothing less. In that moment, Jay knew he had to work with this man.

The following day, Jay shifted his specialty from orthopedic surgery to ophthalmologic surgery. Dr. Nordan generously shared his brilliance, experience and skills with everyone he touched—including Jay as they were together at the Eye Institute until Dr. Nordan's passing in 2015.

Every Monday, eight guys met in the lounge at Jay's office after everyone else had gone home. Jay and Brian Taub had started the group as an office league, joined by founding partner Dr. Scott

Silverman and three residents. They needed two more people to fill in the minimum of eight, so they invited two geeky friends from college days, Ron Patel and Don Elias, to join them. Ron ran a software company from his spare bedroom, and Don worked a bank of monitors in Loss Prevention at a major retail chain.

Inseparable friends, they couldn't appear more different. Ron Patel was dark with long sideburns and a fat moustache. He had a wife, two small children, and a spacious home in the suburbs.

Don had springy red hair, his face covered with freckles. Closing in on thirty years old, he looked to be about sixteen. He drove a 2003 Hyundai Elantra with peeling paint. He rented a downstairs apartment from his mother who lived upstairs.

Setting up for the evening, Jay opened pizza boxes while Brian pulled plastic containers of sushi from a large paper bag. Brian and Scott kept kosher so sushi was a good option for takeout. Don connected his laptop to the big screen TV. He always lined out a montage of plays by key players from the week.

At the beginning of the season, everyone put $100 into a pool. Whoever won the Super Bowl got the pool just in time for the holidays.

"How's the Big Day coming along?" Brian asked Jay as they filled their plates.

Jay groaned.

"That good?" Brian snorted. "It happens to the best of us, man."

"You married Jewish," Jay said, reproachfully. "My mother…"

Brian cut him off. "Stop right there. I know the whole story without another word. Save us both the pain."

"You guys think you're the only ones who have wedding troubles?" Don Patel asked, filling a red cup with cola. "My mother refused to come out of the dressing room for the wedding because my wife's Methodist, not Hindi. We started an hour late."

"What did you do?" Jay asked, pausing.

"The officiant had to go in a coax her out," Don said. "He finally got through to her when he asked her if this is how she wanted to be remembered when someone thinks of her son's wedding day."

"It wasn't any picnic for me either," Brian said. After briefly dating Hillie's friend Sally Wilson, Brian had married Hannah, a Jewish girl. "Between her mother and mine—we both had our hands full."

Still at the food table, Scott Silverman chuckled. The old man of the group, he was on the verge of retirement. "I wish I could say you'll only do it once, guys. You should be so lucky." Scott was on his third wife.

Ron switched on the big screen and talk turned to football.

Later that week, Jay and Hillie visited a beach wedding venue. They were on their way back to L.A. when Hillie threw her journal onto the backseat of the car and sagged in her seat. She was so tired of driving and even more tired of thinking. They rode in Jay's Mercedes today. Hillie called it the most boring car in the world—gray inside and outside. "After going to Rancho Las Cruces, every place seems tame," she said.

Turning down the music, Jay glanced at her and placed his hand on hers. "How do you feel about the resort now that we're away from it? Is it still in the running for the wedding?"

"I love it," she said. "Rancho Las Cruces will probably be one of our favorite vacation spots from now on, but for the wedding…" Her voice became doubtful. "I'm thinking of the travel expense for our guests, plus the time it takes to get there…"

He focused on driving as they approached a slow-moving SUV.

"On the other hand, think of the fabulous wedding pictures…" she said.

"Think of the cost to fly the photographer in to take the wedding pictures," Jay finished.

"I'm not crossing Rancho Las Cruces off as a possibility," Hillie said. "Eventually I'll make a list of the pros and cons for each location, and we can decide."

He glanced at her, his voice mellow. "Hillie, can I make a suggestion?"

"Sure." She rested her head on the back of her seat and turned to look at him.

"Forget the lists and the cost-benefit analysis, okay? Just go with your heart."

She gave him a soft smile. "I knew there was a reason to keep you around."

He caressed her face with the back of his hand.

The following week, Rabbi Sam had a wedding at Gershon Bachus Vintners in Temecula Valley. Jay couldn't get away from the office, but Hillie left Becca with a list and clear instructions and hurried away from the studio shortly before 2:00 p.m. to get ahead of traffic for the ninety-minute drive. She had to attend this wedding and get a look at the winery. The new set design wouldn't implode if she disappeared for three hours.

Even after all the driving and touring these past few weeks, Hillie was looking forward to the afternoon. Temecula would always have special meaning to her.

Dust billowed behind her car as she wound around the hillsides up the long gravel lane to the winery. She pulled into the parking lot as Rabbi Sam was getting out of his car. He waved and walked over.

"Good afternoon!" he said, giving her a brief hug. "Great to see you."

"Tell me something good," Hillie said brightly.

"Today we have an orthodox wedding. Dan and Yardena."

"I don't think I've ever been to an orthodox wedding before," Hillie told him.

"We're broadening your horizons," Rabbi Sam said, with his signature smile. "Feel free to cruise around and explore the facility. This is a gorgeous venue—family owned and operated. I'll introduce you to Kenny and Christina. They live upstairs here."

Surrounded by rolling hills, Gershon Bachus Vintners stood on a summit crowned by its massive building of cream-colored stucco with a clay tile roof. Iron balconies fronted several French windows on the second story. Hillie had the feeling she might be back in Tuscany. She had traveled with her father to Europe or Asia every summer from the time she was fifteen, all the way through college.

Grapevines, orchards and farms in the distance—she drew in a deep breath. These fragrances fed the soul. What a lovely place for an outdoor wedding.

And the pictures…

While Rabbi Sam stayed busy with his wedding preparations, Hillie climbed some stone stairs along the building and drew up. The wrought-iron dome with the GBV insignia over the gazebo, white rose bushes, yellow wooden folding chairs—this was the exact scene they had passed over while Jay proposed.

Wow. Now they had her attention.

Blue hydrangeas and white roses filled hanging baskets on both sides of the aisle, with more hydrangeas and white roses on the posts of the Chuppah and the Greek columns supporting the dome. A white runner ran the entire length of the walkway.

A white satin ribbon cordoned off the seating area. Hillie circled the building to see a covered patio made up of square pavers in various tones from deep orange to blue. Strings of twinkle lights surrounded the space. She stepped through an open door and found herself in the reception hall. Overhead, golden fabric draped across the ceiling Mediterranean style.

On each side of the hall, four oversized garage doors could slide up to make this a perfect indoor-outdoor venue. Hillie pulled out her phone to get pictures. Jay had to see this.

Behind her, the bakery crew gathered their equipment to make a discreet getaway. On one end of the long table a six-layer white cake had a blue swag studded with pearls diagonally across its entire length. The other end of the table held row upon row of half-pint jars filled with four varieties of cake in a glass. The names Yardena and Dan were engraved on everything imaginable.

Hillie kept snapping pictures until music and a group of people laughing outside brought her back to earth. What time was it now? She glanced at her cell phone and hurried outside.

Bouncing with excitement, Yardena had the center seat in a row of seven chairs on the edge of the patio outside. The other chairs held several women of all ages. A clapping crowd stood around the edges of the patio. Someone played a violin. Yardena wore a simple lace-covered gown with a high neckline and dangling pearl earrings. A pearl tiara framed her dark hair with a filmy organza veil wafting behind her.

Within minutes, Dan arrived arm in arm with his parents along with about thirty boisterous friends. He wore a dark suit with a white shirt, white bow tie and white yarmulke. His brown hair bristled in a military cut.

He approached Yardena, bent close to her and whispered something. Their faces glowed as they gazed into each other's eyes. Moving slowly, he pulled the top layer of the veil forward to cover her face. More cheers. Laughing, Yardena blew him kisses.

Enjoying the moment, Rabbi Sam stood near the end of the line of seated women. He caught sight of Hillie and nodded, smiling.

Wearing a blue yarmulke with white trim, his tallit draped around his shoulders, he looked very dignified.

Dan and party headed around the building with almost everyone following them, except the bridesmaids and a few others. Hillie stayed near the back of the jostling, cheering crowd. When they rounded the corner to the ceremony location, she found a seat near the aisle two rows from the back.

Jay had been right. The Las Cruces wedding had been tame. This was a real celebration—noisy and fun. She couldn't help laughing with them.

Rabbi Sam took his place at the front of the Chuppah as the guests found seats on the folding chairs. More than a hundred people had turned out for the event. Before long, the groom and his parents arrived. He entered the Chuppah to put on a long white garment over his suit and button it up. The groomsmen lined up outside the Chuppah, facing the guests.

The music, the bridesmaids' entrance music… finally, Yardena appeared with her parents. They paused a few feet from the front. Her mother held Yardena for a moment then released her. The dad hugged his daughter like he'd never let her go, then kissed her cheek. He wiped his face and took a seat next to his wife.

The bride took the last three steps to reach Dan. Someone handed each of them an orchid. Yardena offered the flower to Dan's mother, followed by a hug. Dan gave the orchid to Yardena's mother. At that point more than a dozen tissues appeared across the crowd.

Dan took Yardena's hand, and they moved under the Chuppah. Yardena circled Dan seven times, and they shared a glass of wine.

Rabbi Sam said, "This is a place where nature and G-d meet and do a dance. We will never all be together the same way as we are today." Holding a printout, he read the Ketubah, then the groom placed a simple gold wedding band on Yardena's index finger. Smiling and triumphant, she held it up to show the guests.

At that point, several people walked forward holding printed pages to read the Seven Blessings. Hillie copied some of them into her journal. She would definitely include this tradition in their wedding.

Rabbi Sam held up a glass of wine. "Send your good wishes for Dan and Yardena into the glass," he said. He handed the glass to Dan who again drank and shared the glass with Yardena. He folded the veil back from her face.

Rabbi Sam placed a cloth bundle on the ground, and Dan stamped it with his heel. POP.

"*Mazel Tov!*" Cheering, the guests stood as the couple kissed and headed toward the back. The entire ceremony had taken twenty-two and a half minutes, just like Rabbi Sam had said.

The bridal couple retreated down the center aisle and up the stairs into the building. The guests began milling around, hugging and congratulating family members.

On his way past her, Rabbi Sam paused. "I've been invited to stay for the reception. Would you like to stay as my guest?"

"Thank you, but I have to get back."

He nodded. "We have about thirty minutes before the bride and groom come out. They'll go to a private room to rest and have something to eat. I want to introduce you to Kenny and Christina, the owners, before you go."

Hillie walked with him to the covered patio. "They put on a cocktail hour before serving the food," he told her.

The outdoor bar had a crowd around it. Servers wearing black smocks carried giant trays loaded with hors d'oeuvres—mini cupcake quiches, sliced cucumbers topped with veggies, and the cutest little shooter glasses half filled with tomato soup with a triangle of grilled cheese standing in the glass.

Hillie asked the server to stand still so she could take a close-up photo of those shooter glasses. This was fun. She tasted the soup and sandwich. Crispy, buttery... Yummy.

"That's imitation cheese," Rabbi Sam told her. "This is a kosher reception. We're having sirloin later."

"You're kidding!" Hillie said, savoring the final taste. "It's so good."

He stepped toward the bar area where the crowd had thinned down a little. "Dan and Yardena chose to have a wine-tasting bar. Gershon Bachus has the only kosher-style wine in the country." He reached around the side of the bar and picked up a bottle for her to see it. "They can even private label the bottles for the wedding."

The label read, Yardena and Dan with the date. Nice. She made a note. "Guests can purchase these bottles as mementoes," he told her. He reached for a wine glass and handed it to her. "Take a sip."

"Just a sip. I'm driving." She tasted. "Uhmmm... That's phenomenal. So smooth."

"That's what everyone says!" He grinned. "I love this place." He looked across the patio. "Oh, there's Christina now. She's coming out of the Reception Room."

Petite with blond hair and bangs, Christina wore a blue sequined dress. She was that eye-catching combination of athletic and feminine. When she caught sight of Rabbi Sam, her face lit up, and she stepped toward them.

"Christina, I'd love for you to meet Hillie Gordon," Rabbi Sam said, when she reached them. "She's here as my guest to take a look at the venue and watch me in action."

Christina held out her hand to Hillie. "Welcome. We're delighted to have you here." Her eyes sparkled.

Hillie instantly liked her. "Your place is incredible," Hillie said. "I'm seeing so much attention to detail in every single area."

"It's our lifelong dream come true," Christina said, gazing around. "Gershon Bachus was Kenny's grandfather. He came over from the Ukraine with his special recipes for making fine wine with a dream of having his own family winery someday." She gazed at the rows of grape vines outside near the patio. "I like to believe he's here is spirit, watching over us."

With warmth rising from her heart, Hillie nodded. "I believe that."

A server paused near them, and Rabbi Sam took a tiny quiche from the tray. "These are so good. Try one." He passed one to Hillie.

Christina said, "Since this is a kosher reception, they brought in a kosher caterer. Most of the time, we have a gourmet chef who prepares our food."

"Their chef is gifted," Rabbi Sam confirmed. "His filet mignon will make you want to cry for joy. Once his plates come out of the kitchen, a moment of silence falls across the room."

Christina laughed. "Everyone's too busy eating to say anything. Happens every time!"

"Christina is also the wedding planner, so if you decide to have your wedding here, you'll get Christina as well."

Hillie's eyebrows raised. "Wonderful. I'm a movie set designer, so I just assumed I'd do the wedding planning myself. But it's becoming almost impossible with my job obligations. Not enough hours in a day."

Christina nodded. "That's what most people say. We only host one wedding here per week, so our guests get very personalized attention. I also close the tasting room on the day of the wedding. Let's sit down together soon and talk about how Kenny and I can help you." She touched Rabbi Sam's sleeve. "You're in good hands, Hillie. Rabbi Sam is our absolute favorite here."

"That's what I tell everyone when I mention Gershon Bachus, Christina," Rabbi Sam said, his blue eyes twinkling.

Something caught Christina's attention across the patio. "Let's get together," she said, shaking Hillie's hand again. "Rabbi Sam can set up an appointment where we can all talk. Bring your fiancé." With a parting wave, she hurried away.

"See what I mean?" Rabbi Sam said with personal pride. "I'm their resident rabbi. I come here every week to bless the kosher-style wine. Kenny and Christina are like family. They will be to you, too, if you decide to have your wedding here."

Hillie laughed. "You're convincing me. Keep talking!" She snagged her second grilled cheese shooter. "I've got to go before I spoil my dinner." She popped the bread into her mouth and chewed for a moment. "Jay and I have a date for Chinese tonight. I've got to run." She set her empty glass on a nearby wine barrel set up with a tray for that purpose.

"We'll coordinate calendars by email," Rabbi Sam said. "How about next Sunday? That seems to be the easiest day to get away."

She nodded, brushing off her hands. "That should work. I'll check with Jay this evening and text you."

"Perfect." His Clark Kent glasses glinted from the string lights overhead.

Hillie paused. "How about if we have dinner one evening, at my apartment? Jay and I eat together about three nights a week at my place. After we meet with Christina, it would be great if you could join us, then we can be comfortable to go over everything together."

"Sounds like a plan." He gave her a quick hug. "Safe trip home."

"It's only an hour and a half drive," she said. "Lots of pluses come with this venue." With a wave good-bye, she hurried to her car.

The drive took almost three hours in rush hour. Jay met her outside the restaurant. He loved Chinese, so tonight they were slumming at a dilapidated vegan Chinese buffet with the absolute best food around. Neither Jay nor Hillie were vegan. They just loved the food here.

As soon as Hillie reached Jay, she stepped into his arms, savoring the restful feeling of leaning against him. This day seemed so long, and it wasn't over yet. He didn't press her with talk, giving her a moment to catch her breath before they went inside. Another thing she loved about this man.

When they settled down at their booth with their brimming plates, he asked, "How was the wedding?" A pot of hot tea and two cups waited for them.

Hillie poured tea for both of them. "Honey, I think this might be the place we've been looking for. Gershon Bachus feels so comfortable, and it is absolutely gorgeous." She set down the teapot and leaned forward. "You'll never believe what I'm going to tell you!"

He reached for his cup, watching her and waiting.

"Remember seeing the lawn set up for a wedding at the very moment when you proposed?"

"Sure."

"That's the place! That's Gershon Bachus Vintners!"

His mouth sagged open. "You're kidding." Leaning in, his brows drew together. "You're kidding, right?"

"Nope." She sipped tea. "I thought it was a dream when I got to their backyard, but it was very real."

"What about the facility? Is it good?"

"The best. It's a family-owned winery—pristine and immaculate— but homey at the same time."

"Like you!" He grinned at her mouth-twisting expression.

"I have brochures in my purse, but I want to eat first." She pulled out her cell phone. "Are you good for an appointment this Sunday? Rabbi Sam is setting up a meeting with Christina, the owner, who also happens to be a wedding planner, by the way."

"Sure. Sunday is all yours."

She sent a quick text to Rabbi Sam, then turned off her phone. "I took tons of pictures. We can look at them later. My brain sounds like a beehive inside. Right now, I want to eat and relax." She picked up her fork and speared a giant imitation shrimp. "How was your day? Tell me something good!"

"I think I found a rental house," he said, pulling out his cell phone. He flicked to a certain screen. "What do you think?"

She took the phone from him and scrolled through a dozen photos. "Nice. I love hardwood, and the bathroom looks like it was just updated."

"Glass shower enclosures…" he said, grinning at her with his eyes wide.

She shook her head, in a mock warning. "How much, *Jock*?"

When he told her, she ran through the photos again. "The address says Glendora. Are you okay with that?"

"It will only be until we can find a place to buy. I can deal with the commute for a while."

She handed the phone back to him. "Let's take a look at it."

"We're on for Tuesday after work," he said.

She nodded. "Can't interrupt Monday night Fantasy Football, can we? Okay, Tuesday works for me."

"Great!" He picked up his water glass. "Before we push pause on wedding plans, can we talk about something for just a moment?"

She waited form him to go on. Whatever it was, it must be important for Jay to bring it up now.

"Can we check out one more venue before we decide?"

"Sure. What do you have in mind?"

"Puerto Vallarta."

Something in the tone of his voice made Hillie hesitate. "What brought that up now?" she asked.

"It gets rave reviews online."

She reached for her phone. "Were you thinking of spending a weekend there? I've already taken so much time off…"

"Nothing that drastic," he said. "I was thinking of an overnight trip on a weekend. We could fly down on a Saturday and look around on Sunday, maybe talk to a couple of event planners and come back Sunday night. Would that be okay?"

She nodded and put her phone down. "I'll connect with Rabbi Sam and move our meeting back."

He drew a breath. "Good. This trip is on me. I'll take care of all the reservations." He raised his hand. "Plans officially paused… starting now." He pressed an imaginary button in the air.

Gershon Bachus Vintners

Between San Diego and Los Angeles, Gershon Bachus Vintners is an exclusive, private fine-wine producing estate in the Temecula Valley. Set atop a hill with stunning 360-degree views of the surrounding mountains, their lavishly landscaped ceremonial grounds and cocktail patio offer a dream location for the perfect outdoor wedding.

Gershon Bachus immigrated to the United States from the Ukraine in 1922 with his wife and two girls. He brought with him a zest for life and love for making fine wine. Like many transplanted Europeans, he continued to make wine for his friends and family but never realized his vision of owning his own vineyard in California.

Eighty-four years later, Gershon's grandson, Ken, and his wife, Christina, brought the family dream to life. Their winemaking tradition now lives on in Temecula, California, where they capture the lifestyle described in the many stories from the old country, where family, friends and food come together. While honoring their heritage, Gershon Bachus Vintners stays on the cutting edge with technology that will eventually make their vineyard sustainable and their wine organic.

Gershon Bachus Vintners is the perfect estate for an exclusive affair. Its private Bridal Room has French doors leading directly to the ceremony. Guests can enjoy the ceremony while taking in breathtaking views of the neighboring vineyards and mountains. After the ceremony, the wedding guests move to the covered outdoor patio adjacent to Grenache vines for a cocktail hour. They will socialize with appetizers and beverages while taking in the sun as it sets over the vines.

Once the bride and groom are ready to be announced, guests will be directed to the Reception Room to toast, dine and dance. An exclusive gourmet chef is on call to prepare five-star meals for events at Gershon Bachus Vintners. For more information visit www.GershonBachus.com.

Kosher Wine vs. Kosher-style Wine™

Wine has a different kosher standard than all other food products. In order for wine to be kosher the ingredients, machinery, processing, and the workers have to be observant according to Jewish Law. Gershon Bachus Vintners meets the first three standards. The wine tastes fabulous. However, the workers, the rabbi, and the owners are all non-observant non-Orthodox Jews. Therefore, the wine they produce is kosher-style, and not kosher. Moses would have drunk this wonderful tasting wine, made by G-d and blessed by Rabbi Marc. In Bible days, only Biblical law existed, not rabbinical law. Most all wine is kosher by Biblical standards, but not according to Rabbinical Jewish Law, called Halacha.

The Jewish religion centers on separation and distinction—separating meat from dairy, Shabbat from workdays—but foremost separating Jews from non-Jews: "the people shall dwell alone, and shall not be reckoned among the nations," (Numbers 23:9), a verse every observant Jew knows. For example, over the centuries the simple rule "Thou shalt not seethe a kid in his mother's milk" (Exodus 23:19) evolved into complete separation of any meat product from any dairy product—including separate kitchen sinks, eating hours and utensils.

As for wine, the question of its kashrut ("kosherness") has also evolved over the centuries until a non-Jew or a non-observant Jew touching a container of wine would make the wine lose its kashrut. Thus, the fourth standard—concerning which people have contact with the wine—is the only element missing from Gershon Bachus Vintners' Kosher-style Wine™. Gershon Bachus Vintners produced this wine under Rabbi Marc Rubenstein's rabbinical authorization using a special approved yeast. He arrives at the winery weekly to bless this delicious wine. Gershon Bachus Vintners owns the trademark of Kosher-style Wine™ and invites everyone to try it. Visit www.GershonBachus.com for more information.

Chapter 5

Hotel Playa Fiesta

I look into your eyes and I see the G-d in me,
in the G-d of you.

~ Amanda, in her wedding vows
(taken from Yoga and Orthodox Judaism)

On her way to work the next morning, Hillie called Rabbi Sam before her feet hit the carpet beside her bed. She'd slept in until 9:00. Unheard of. She wore a yellow shirt with LA Lakers in purple across the front, way oversized and very comfy.

"Jay wants us to visit Puerto Vallarta before we settle on the venue," she told Rabbi Sam when he picked up.

He chuckled. "That's interesting," he said. "I have a wedding in Puerto Vallarta coming up in a couple of weeks. How about if I make arrangements for you and Jay to be there?"

"Really?" she said. "That's kind of freaky. Jay brought it up out of the blue last night."

"It's not so unusual. I officiate a few weddings there every year. Beautiful location. You should see it."

"Jay is taking care of the details this time," she said. "I'll let him know to touch base with you on it."

"In that case," Rabbi Sam said, "let's move our next in-person meeting to afterward, okay? I want to wait until you're ready to decide on the venue, so we can make more progress while we're together... unless you and Jay would like to see me right away. I'm always available to you."

"We're good," Hillie said. "No need for a meeting right now. I'll text you Jay's number so you'll have it on your phone. Thank you, Rabbi Sam."

"You are so welcome, Hillie. You're giving me a chance to do what I love."

After they said good-bye, she called Jay and gave him the update. "So... we have the weekend to ourselves," she announced.

"No! That can't be so." He laughed. "There must be something we could do besides relaxing and resting. A museum marathon... or an outlet-mall chase... What do you think?"

"I vote for sitting on my sofa and binge watching the entire five seasons of *Remington Steele*. The DVD pack has been on my bookshelf for 2 years, and I've never seen it."

"With pizza, beer, and ice cream?" he asked.

"Yep."

"I'm in! See you in a few..." He hung up without saying good-bye.

She laughed as she dropped her cell phone to the nightstand. Heading for a quick shower, she had on her sweats and was drying her hair when he rang her doorbell. These were the moments she lived for.

Tuesday evening, they visited the rental property Jay had found. It was even better in person—two bedrooms with a separate man cave and a traffic flow that was made for entertaining. The plan was for Jay to rent the house and move in as soon as it became available, which was January 1, six weeks away.

Another to-do item ticked off their list. If only the wedding were this easy.

Jay took care of the reservations for Puerto Vallarta the following week. A few Saturdays later, he arrived at Hillie's apartment at 8:30 a.m. to pick her up for their flight.

She held her steaming curling iron a safe distance away, as she opened the door. "Want some coffee?" she asked.

He kissed her cheek, avoiding the hot device. "Thanks. I already had some, but more is always better." In three strides he had the carafe in hand.

"Unplug the machine when you're done," she said, on her way back to the bathroom. "I'll be finished here in five minutes."

"We're staying at the Hotel Playa Fiesta," he called after her. "You're going to love it."

Hillie didn't answer him. She was working hard to stay upbeat about this trip. If it weren't that Jay seemed to have his heart set on going, she would have asked him to cancel. She had just been through a killer week finishing up a series of twelve sets for a production, and she started a new project on Wednesday.

On board the plane, she lifted the arm rest between them and leaned on Jay's shoulder. He slouched down until his head rested on the back of his seat. After a little shuffling to get comfortable, Hillie's eyes drifted closed.

A bustling resort city, Puerto Vallarta lay halfway down the Pacific Coast of Mexico. On the same latitude as Hawaii, it had an average temperature of seventy-seven degrees with little rainfall. Water sports, night life, and five-star hotels—the perfect place for a great time.

A few hours later, they set off from the airport in an orange-and-black taxi to drive down the coastal highway for thirty minutes.

Taking in the hillside vistas of the city, Hillie murmured, "I've been here before, Jay. See that?" She pointed to a bridge. "I've seen that before—probably with my father when I was a little girl. But I can't recall the actual trip."

"My parents came here on their honeymoon," Jay said.

Hillie turned to look at him. He was busy gazing out the other side of the car.

"What's our itinerary?" she asked. "I feel out of the loop. Usually I'm the one with the schedule."

He pulled out his phone. "No service," he said, putting it away. "When we get connected, I can pull it up. Off the top of my head…

"We'll stop somewhere and have a nice late lunch, then do some sightseeing. Settle into the hotel, have dinner at their upscale restaurant this evening, maybe end the day with a walk on the beach." He grinned at her. "Tracking with me so far?" he asked.

She nodded. "You're doing good, Jock. Keep going."

"At 9:00 tomorrow morning, we meet with the event planner for a tour of our hotel as a possible venue. After that we visit two more hotels before Rabbi Sam's wedding begins at 4:00, then back to the airport to fly out tomorrow evening."

"I wonder if they have a masseuse at the hotel," she said. "That would be so amazing."

Known as the friendliest town in Mexico, Puerto Vallarta is the San Francisco of the Mexican West Coast, with a large bay and plenty of shopping, food, and drink. Busy and bustling, the contrast to Rancho Las Cruces was striking.

A little before 3:00 p.m. they arrived at The Hotel Playa Fiesta, definitely festive with its lush banks of bougainvilleas in brilliant orange, lavender and pink.

Inside the lobby, white-washed plaster, terrazzo floors, and arched doorways brought up a feeling of serene luxury. Sunlight shone through the glass doors to the back.

While Jay checked in, Hillie wandered outside. The back terrace stretched out to the beachfront. While Jay was checking in, Hillie strolled outside, past the two pools, to the edge of the deck. The coastline here was untouched. Raw nature—lovely and rich—stretched out on both sides of the hotel.

"Hillie?" Jay called from the door. "I've got our keys."

She hurried inside. "What about the masseuse?"

A boutique hotel, the structure stood four stories high. Their room was on the second floor. More white washed walls with beige marble floor tiles—so restful after a day's travel. And, even better, Hillie managed to get a massage before dinner.

"I'm glad we don't have anywhere special to go tonight," she told Jay over filet mignon and lobster. "Sorry to be a downer, but I'm really tired. You go ahead, but I'm going to skip the swim." She sipped cabernet sauvignon.

"No rules here," he said, smiling into her eyes. "We've been on a mad dash for weeks. No wonder you're exhausted."

"I'm glad this is the last trip for a while," she said.

Feeling the delicious effects of the massage and the wine, she was sound asleep before Jay finished his shower and didn't move for ten hours.

The next morning, Hillie stepped onto the sunlit balcony and breathed in the ocean breeze. She wore a yellow cotton sundress and white sandals. Her hair was wrapped into a tight ball with two chopsticks holding it together. Closing her eyes, she leaned her head back, automatically going into Sun Salutation yoga pose—hands outstretched and back as far as she could bend. It felt so good.

When she relaxed and let her arms drop, Jay came behind her and wrapped his arms around her. "Happy?" he asked.

She snuggled back against his blue tee-shirt. "I can't believe we're in the middle of a city," she said. "It feels so peaceful here."

"You missed the most amazing sunset. The sky was on fire and so was the sea. It was incredible."

"Sorry. I'm glad I was sleeping! Maybe we can find a postcard of it."

He tickled her side and she arched her back, giggling.

"Let's get some breakfast," he said. "Last night's dinner is long gone."

"Look!" Hillie watched four staff members decorating the terrace for the wedding.

"Let's look later," he said, taking her hand. "We've got an hour until we meet with the event planner. Let's go!"

She snagged her purse on the way to the door.

When they returned fifty minutes later, Rabbi Sam was chatting with the resident wedding planner, a dark-haired woman wearing a white dress with a red scarf around her neck. Rabbi Sam introduced her as Lindsay Burges, the hotel owner. She was about the same size as Hillie.

Smiling, she said, "Are you ready to look around? We can talk about the details after we finish the tour."

They moved to the terrace containing two curved pools. One of them had a little island with tiny thatched roof with room enough for two people to stand.

Lindsay nodded toward the island. "Our wedding couples like to stand there and get their pictures taken."

"How do they get out there?" Hillie asked.

Lindsay smiled. "We have our ways." She led them toward a long narrow outdoor room to the right. A Chuppah stood at one end of the space with chairs set up and a center aisle.

"Here's where the weddings take place," Lindsay said. She gestured toward the waves. "You can see we have a stretch of unpopulated beach here. Great for pictures."

"This is cozy," Hillie said. "I love the feel of the ocean so close." She lifted her face to catch the wind.

They moved to a table near the pool, and Lindsay handed Hillie a folder. "Here are the packages and the options," she said. "Let's sit down and take a look, shall we?"

"What about the food?" Jay asked. "My family keeps kosher."

She opened her notebook and drew out a leaflet. "We work with a kosher caterer in the area. Here is their contact information and the menu. Their Challah is the best, from what I'm told."

Jay nodded, glanced over the leaflet and handed it to Hillie. She slipped it into the folder. Jay shook hands with Lindsay. "Thank you. We'll take a look at these. Sorry to have to rush away, but we've got another appointment in less than an hour."

Rabbi Sam stood. "Thank you, Lindsay. We won't hold you up any longer. You've got a busy day ahead of you." When she hurried away, he said, "See you at four, kids. Three-thirty if you want to be here for the Bedeken." With a wave, he went back inside.

Hillie and Jay followed at a slower pace and found a taxi at the curb—a scuffed sedan with ragged seats. Jay opened the door for Hillie and called out the address to the driver. Walking could be treacherous as there were no sidewalks.

When they were on their way, Hillie opened the folder Lindsay had given her. "This is actually a pretty good deal," she said. "Five-hour open bar, decorations included, live music, the wedding cake... and it includes a bridal suite with champagne. Pretty much everything, from what I'm seeing."

"Do you think it's a possibility as a venue?" he asked.

She bobbed her head from side to side. "Maybe. I would add it to my benefit analysis spreadsheet, but that's off the table."

He laughed and put his arm around her.

Their next appointment went well, but the cost was way out of their price range.

The last hotel was an immediate no. Once lavish with wide columns and mosaic murals, the building had cracked floors and a ceiling stained from water damage. The chandeliers had missing crystals, their metal parts pitted with age.

Jay gave an excuse at the front desk, and they quickly escaped to do a little shopping instead.

Shortly after 2:00 p.m. they returned to their hotel. In their room, Hillie kicked off her sandals, pulled the pillow up behind her, and sat against the headboard with her bare feet stretched out on the bedspread, leafing through the print materials from the day.

Jay opened the small refrigerator. "Want a water bottle?" he asked, offering her one.

"Thanks!" She opened the lid and took a long drink. "So, your parents came to Puerto Vallarta on their honeymoon?" she asked.

Jay plopped down beside her and picked up a pamphlet. "Mom has an entire picture album full of photos, mostly of her and Dad at the beach."

"Did they stay at the Playa Fiesta?" she went on.

"No. The last hotel we visited." He sipped his drink. "The dilapidated one."

Hillie let the folder slide to the bed. She focused on Jay. "Okay… Tell me what this is really about…"

He looked up, wary. "It's a beautiful location," he said. "Don't you think so?"

"It's lovely," she agreed. "What I've seen so far is wonderful. But I'm getting the feeling there was another reason why you suggested coming down here." She bore in on him. "Your mother is behind this, isn't she?"

His face turned red. He stared at the pamphlet in his hands.

"Jay, I'm so disappointed. I thought we told each other everything." She scrambled off the bed.

"Hillie. Please don't get upset." He stood up, his hands stretched out to her.

She backed away. "What do you expect?" She let out a quick sigh. "Tell me the truth, the whole truth, and nothing but the truth. Now."

His shoulders sagged. "Mom has been hounding me for weeks about having the wedding down here."

Hillie's mouth formed an oval.

Before she could speak, he said, "Not that I expected you to go for it. I just wanted to be able to tell her that we came and looked at it. Now I can go home and tell her it was too expensive, or too small… or something. Just to get her off my back." He raked his fingers through his curls. "I'm sorry, Hillie." He looked completely dejected.

Her heart softened. She slipped into his arms. "It's okay. I'm not mad anymore." She hugged him, then stepped back. Her expression grew intense. "But this is the last time. Don't ever do this again. Promise?"

He nodded.

She went on. "I know you're in a tough spot, and I want to work with you to make things as easy for you as I can. But you have to be honest with me."

He looked down, tension in his voice. "I guess I'm not used to it… telling everything, I mean. In our family, we avoid conflict by withholding information. I know that's not healthy. We had to go through counseling classes in med school, and that's something I learned then. But putting it into practice terrifies me. When you get mad at me, I feel like I'm going to have a heart attack or a stroke or something."

She moved closer to meet his gaze. "I know this isn't easy for you. One of the main problems is you're so adorable. You want to keep everyone happy. So do I. But when so many conflicting opinions pile up, there's no way to keep everyone happy. It's impossible."

He hugged her close and drew in a long breath. She rested against him. This was home.

When Jay spoke again, his words sounded ragged. "I never want to be without you, Hillie. I can't imagine it."

Tears came to her eyes. "That's what we're here for," she said. "Till death do us part, remember?"

His arms tightened around her. "Even that seems too short."

The room went silent for a long moment. Sounds of laughing and talking came from the terrace below.

"Tell you what," Hillie murmured. "How about if we stay up here and watch the wedding from our bird's eye view? We can see everything from the balcony."

"Great idea!" Jay said, kissing her. "In that case, we won't have to dress up. And we can get our stuff together, too. We need to leave here by 5:30 in order to make our flight."

After 10:00 that evening, Hillie had hardly dropped her suitcase in her living room when her phone chirped. She flicked the screen.

"Hi, Dad!" she said. "Is everything all right? I just got back from Puerto Vallarta."

"Still hunting for your wedding venue?" he asked. "Tell me something good!"

"It's all good. I'm really tired of all the traveling to find the perfect spot, though. Jay and I have taken a couple of mini-vacations while looking. That's the good kind of multi-tasking."

Larry Gordon chuckled. His voice had a light quality she hadn't heard in years. "I called because I have some news of my own."

"Tell me something good," she said, her heart stepping up its pace. Something told her this was going to be big.

"I'm seeing someone," he said.

Hillie sank to her bed. She tried to keep her tone light. "Great, Dad! I'm so happy for you."

"She's a wonderful woman, Hillie. I can't wait for you to meet her." He chuckled again. "We've actually worked in the same office for five years. A couple of months ago I sort of woke up and realized she was there."

Hillie waited for him to go on. She couldn't find her voice right now.

He paused. When she didn't reply he plowed ahead. "Her name is Dorothy Fein and—you'll never guess!—she's Jewish!"

"Is she observant?"

"No. Her husband was Anglican. She hasn't practiced Judaism since she was a girl."

"When can I meet her?" Hillie asked.

"We were thinking of getting together with you and Jay soon. What are your weekends like between now and Thanksgiving?"

"We're done traveling, so I'll have to check with Jay, but I think any weekend will do."

"Great. How about next Saturday? We'll go out to dinner at Giorgio's, the four of us. Next Saturday at, say, 7:00?"

"I'll check with Jay," Hillie breathed. "Tomorrow I'll confirm with you on that, okay?"

"Wonderful!" he said.

Why did he sound so giddy?

"Oh, and one thing you need to know," he said, growing more serious. "She's African-American."

Hillie considered herself as open minded as anyone in California, but she felt a jolt. "I'm looking forward to meeting her," she said, trying to sound natural. "Anyone who can catch your eye after all this time has to be someone special."

"She is!" he said.

They said good-bye shortly afterward. Hillie immediately called Jay.

"Are you sitting down?" she asked him when he picked up. "Life just got interesting."

Hotel Playa Fiesta in Puerto Vallarta

Puerto Vallarta dates back to the 1700s with its old town feel, small cobblestone streets and wonderful restaurants and shops at every turn. The Bay of Bandares, one of the deepest in the world, attracts a huge array of wildlife, including the seasonal migration of the humpback whales. With the wonderful vistas created by the uninhabited mountains rising straight out of the water you can find beautiful views wherever you venture.

At Playa Fiesta the pool area is where everything happens. With all your family and friends around, it becomes your own personal backyard party, giving that intimate feeling of being at home. If a beach is what you are looking for, Playa Fiesta sits directly on the water.

The restaurant and bar is adjacent to the pool area. Since 2007, our executive chef Sergio Guzman, has created a wonderful balance of mixed cuisine with a Mexican flare.

Hotel Playa Fiesta's rooms all have that unique villa style feel with individual rooms for privacy or multi bedroom units perfect for families or close friends traveling together. Our wedding terrace overlooks the water.

If you are the adventurous traveler, there are a multitude of activities for you to enjoy in Puerto Vallarta including...

- Snorkeling and SCUBA at Los Arcos
- Deep sea fishing outside of the bay
- Golf and tennis
- Hiking to secluded waterfalls.
- Surf trips to Sayulita
- Whale watching excursions
- Group boat tours with food and drink
- ATV trips into the hills above Vallarta
- Wave runners, paddleboards & parasailing

Chapter 6

The Plan

I am my beloved's and my beloved is mine.

~ Ketubah text

On Saturday, Jay arrived at Hillie's apartment in the late afternoon. She had her wedding folder out with clippings spread out over the dining room table along with the information from the many venues they had visited.

She let him in, pulling the door wide and stepping back to the table while he came inside and closed it behind him.

"How are you doing?" he asked, watching her face. "Ready to meet the new girlfriend?"

She drew in a breath. "Ready as I'll ever be, I guess."

He pulled her into a hug. "Lots of changes for you, babe. It can't be easy."

She pressed her cheek to the side of his face. "Just when I thought I was maxed out on stress." She pulled away to reach for her phone.

"He texted me a picture of the two of them." She pulled the image up and showed it to Jay. "She's beautiful."

He took the phone from her and tilted it for better viewing.

In the photo, Larry Gordon sat on a park bench close to a woman with the hair and coloring of Halle Berry—plus a few years. She had a gentle, wise expression.

"She looks like a really nice person," he said, handing the phone back to her.

"I feel terrible," Hillie said, sinking into her chair at the table. "Dad has been so lonely, and he's found a lovely woman that he's crazy about. I'm such a selfish daughter." She covered her face with one hand. Her voice became shrill. "Why can't I be happy for him, and let it go at that?"

"You and your dad are so close. It's no wonder you're struggling." He knelt in front of her, taking her hand down so he could look into her face. "It's an adjustment, honey. We'll meet… What's her name?"

"Dorothy."

"We'll meet Dorothy tonight, and take it one step at a time. You want your dad to be happy, right?"

"More than anything!"

"Okay. That's the criteria. Does she make him happy? Anything else is a minor detail."

She threw her arms around his neck. "I love you, Jock Jaworski. You are so good for me."

He pulled her close. "I love you, too, soon-to-be Mrs. Jaworski."

They arrived at Giorgio's shortly before 7:00. Larry and Dorothy stood together just inside the doors. She wore a sheath dress in navy blue with a short strand of pearls and low pumps. Stunning.

"Dad!" Hillie went in for a hug.

"Meet Dot," Larry said. "She's been anxious to meet you."

"Hi," Dorothy said, holding out her hand.

Fighting off her awkwardness, Hillie shook hands and introduced Jay.

Following the host to their table, Hillie reached for Jay's hand and realized her own hands were like ice.

"We always get their pastitsio," Jay said as menus appeared.

"You come here often?" Dot asked. She had a peaceful, genuine smile.

"Every few weeks," Jay replied. "And we always get pastitsio."

"It's known as Greek comfort food…" Hillie added, "…for a reason."

Dot closed her menu. "That's what I'm getting."

Larry nodded. "Me too. How are your wedding plans coming along?"

They talked about the various venues Jay and Hillie had visited.

"I'm thinking of wearing Mom's wedding dress," Hillie said. "I've had it in my closet all these years."

"Is it still wearable?" Larry asked.

She nodded. "I have to get an expert opinion, but I think it will work with a little alteration."

"How wonderful to have that," Dot said. "What a treasure." She meant it.

Hillie smiled, interested. "So, how did you meet?" she asked, glancing at Larry and back at Dot.

Dot laughed, her shoulders shaking. She looked slightly guilty.

"She chased me until I caught her," Larry said, laughing with her.

"It happened in the company lounge," Dot said. "And I wasn't doing any chasing, that's for sure."

Larry said, "For the past couple of years…"

Dot held up four fingers.

"For the past *four* years…" he amended, "we've been eating lunch together in the breakroom, maybe two or three days a week. Just casual. Talking about stuff… whatever."

"He helped me so much after my husband passed," Dot said. "He'd been through it too, and that gave us a lot to talk about."

"A couple years ago, we started walking together on lunch break. She was so adamant that she would never marry again that I thought she was safe." He shook his head, eyebrows up in a self-deprecating expression.

"Never say never, right?" Dot said, sharing a glance with him.

Larry said, "We started going to some shows together and a few trips to the beach…"

"We had a non-dating, platonic friendship," Dot said. "I didn't realize how attached we were getting."

"Me neither. Until we went to the convention in September…"

Hillie realized she was leaning forward to catch every word. A warm feeling spread across her chest and upward to her throat. Jay reached for her hand under the table and gave it a gentle squeeze.

The following afternoon, Rabbi Sam arrived at Hillie's apartment holding a bottle of wine with a Gershon Bachus label on it. He handed the bottle to Jay saying, "This is part of my three-step homework: practice kissing, holding hands, and drinking wine."

Grinning, Jay took the bottle. "We've been working on that," he said.

"That's some of the kosher-style wine I mentioned," Rabbi Sam went on. "I brought it so you can share some with your family, Jay. Build some goodwill."

Jay laughed ruefully. "Goodwill is exactly what we need right now." He set the bottle on the kitchen counter.

"Let's sit in the dining area," Hillie interjected, nodding toward the glass-topped round table in the corner. It had a white bowl filled with oranges in the center. "Would you like coffee, Rabbi Sam?"

"Thank you, Hillie. Nothing for me right now." He sat across from Jay. "How are things going with the family?"

"How long do you have?" Hillie asked. "If we get into that, it could take a while."

"I have all the time in the world," Rabbi Sam said. "It's time we talked about this."

Hillie refilled her coffee cup and topped off Jay's. She took her seat as Jay said, "This whole thing with the wedding keeps getting worse and worse."

Hillie added, "We had a fight about it at the Hotel Playa Fiesta. Our first fight about the wedding."

"Is that why you didn't come down for the ceremony?" Rabbi Sam asked.

"We could see everything from our balcony," Jay said. "It was better in about four different ways to watch from up there."

"Beautiful place," Hillie said. "And a gorgeous ceremony."

Rabbi Sam nodded. "For sure. Lovely place. Lovely people." He glanced from one to the other. "So what was the fight about?"

Jay looked at Hillie. "You tell that part, okay?" He looked miserable. Hillie touched his sleeve.

"It turns out Jay's mother has been hounding him to have the wedding in Puerto Vallarta because that's where his parents went on their honeymoon. Jay didn't feel comfortable telling me that when he suggested we visit there. When I found out, I blew up." She sent Jay an upside down smile. "It's the first time we've had secrets. We talk about everything."

"And you got hurt feelings," Rabbi Sam said, waiting for her nod. He turned to Jay. "You're under the gun, Jay. There's no doubt about it. It's a tug of war with your family on one hand, your bride on the other—and you getting stretched in the middle."

Jay said. "My first loyalty is to Hillie. I'm rock solid on that."

"But you love your mother, too," Rabbi Sam finished. He pulled a white legal pad from his case. "Here's what we're going to do." Finding a pen, he said, "Your mother's name is…"

"Olivia."

Writing *How to Make Olivia Happy* on top of the paper, he said, "What's the first thing you can think of that she wants?"

"She wants me to marry a nice Jewish girl," Jay blurted out.

"Of course she does," Rabbi Sam said, "but the fact is sixty-five percent of Jewish people marry a non-Jewish partner. That's the day we live in." He wrote a big number one on the paper. "What's something you can actually do to make her happy?"

Jay looked at the white ceiling tiles. "She keeps talking about the reception, how she's worried she won't be able to eat or drink at her only son's wedding."

"That's good. We can put that to rest quickly enough." He wrote it down. "And kudos to you for taking care of that already. Great thinking." He paused. "What else?"

Over the next ten minutes, they had a list of six items.

"So here's what you're going to do." He tore the page from the legal pad and handed it to Jay. "Go through this list and take steps to relieve Olivia's mind about these points. This is a process, Jay, not a quick fix. We're going to have this conversation several times before the wedding, guaranteed.

"From my experience, I can tell you that most of your mother's fretting is pure anxiety. The more soothing information you can give her, the more she will calm down. Just realize that it won't be perfect—don't expect it to be perfect."

Jay put his hand over Hillie's on the table.

"This is your wedding, the two of you," Rabbi Sam continued. "You have the right to make it meaningful, whatever that looks like to you. Setting realistic expectations on what a good outcome would look like is also part of this process."

Jay said, "I just want to get through the ceremony with everyone still talking to each other."

"Good call," Rabbi Sam said. "That's a good place to start." He leaned back in his chair. "Are we good on that?"

Jay nodded. He folded the paper and slid it into his shirt pocket.

Rabbi Sam said, "So what are you thinking on the venue?"

Hillie leaned over to snatch a printout from under the tea caddy on the counter. She waved it over her head. "Here's my benefit analysis spreadsheet."

Jay grabbed it from her in mid-air. "Your what?" He glanced at the page but didn't have time to read it before Hillie took it back.

She cried out and held it away into the corner behind her. Jay lunged out of his chair. They scuffled for a moment, laughing and shouting.

"You're tearing it!" Hillie gasped, short on breath.

Finally, Jay got the paper from her and sat down, smoothing it out. He gasped and threw it on the table. "That's not about the venues. It's your budget for the set project!"

Hillie wiped her streaming eyes. She pushed her tousled hair out of her face.

Rabbi Sam was laughing with them. "What was that about?" he asked.

Hillie took a breath to calm herself. "I keep saying that I need to make a benefit analysis spreadsheet to decide on the venue. Jay told me to forget about that and go with my heart." She continued speaking to Rabbi Sam, but she leaned forward to stare at Jay. "He's been so serious lately, I thought it would be fun to tweak him a little."

Jay got up to lean over her for a hug. Shaking his head, he took his seat.

Rabbi Sam's blue eyes twinkled. "She's one in a million, Jay. I can see I don't have to tell you that."

They spent the next few minutes discussing the three top runners under consideration for the wedding venue.

Finally, Jay stood and picked up the bottle of wine Rabbi Sam had brought them. "This right here," he turned the label toward Hillie, "is the tipping point as far as I can see."

"Kosher-style wine?" Rabbi Sam asked.

Jay nodded.

"Your mother would love that," Hillie said. "And that's not all. I love the Gershon Bachus winery. It's in a beautiful location, the reception hall is gorgeous, and it's close by—only ninety minutes away."

They looked at each other for a long moment. "Are you thinking what I'm thinking?" Jay asked her.

She nodded. "I don't need a spreadsheet to figure it out." She looked at Rabbi Sam. "It looks like Gershon Bachus Vintners takes the day."

"My only holdback is I've never been there," Jay said, taking his seat.

"I'll set up an appointment with Christina," Rabbi Sam said. He picked up his phone and sent a text message. "She'll get back to me in a few minutes. Maybe we can get that squared away before I leave. Let's get you a full tour of the winery, and a meeting with Christina to talk about what she can do to help with the wedding planning."

"Perfect," Hillie said, beaming at Jay. "This feels right."

He kissed her hand. "Sure does."

With a little schedule shuffling, two days later they drove to Temecula Valley late in the afternoon.

The rolling hills, the vineyards, beautiful farmland in the distance—such a peaceful scene all around them. The vineyards to the south had an earthy, untouched feel. Once they turned into the Gershon Bachus drive, they left the pavement behind. Crunching gravel under their tires, the vines rising on the hillsides—this was real.

"Wow. Look at that view," Jay said, as he drove into the parking area.

"Wait 'till you see it from their yard," Hillie said. She glanced at her phone. "We've got twenty minutes until our appointment with Christina. Let's take a look before we go inside."

They strolled through the grounds with Hillie pointing out the various landmarks—the rose hedge, the doors where the bride and groom had disappeared, the happy-hour patio on the other side.

"They had the Chuppah under the wrought iron dome," she said, turning toward the wide lawn. "And a table under there..."

Jay did a complete turn to see it from every angle. "What do you think? Now that you're seeing it again?" Jay asked. "Still okay?"

She nodded, beaming at him.

"In that case, let's go see the lady."

Christina met them at the front doors. She wore a black polo shirt with GBV insignia and tan twill pants. "Welcome!" She hugged Hillie. "So wonderful seeing you again."

Hillie introduced Jay.

"Rabbi Sam said to tell you hello," Hillie told Christina.

Christina nodded, smiling. "He was here this morning. He comes every week to bless our kosher-style wine. What a lovely man."

They spent the next twenty minutes going through the facility and another twenty walking outside. Finally, Christina led them to a side door. "Let's go inside. I have everything spread out on a table in the tasting room."

The large room felt dim and cool after the brilliant sun.

"Have a seat," Christina said, ushering them toward a long table. Fliers and print-outs covered the center of the table. She handed them each a tri-fold brochure. "Can I get you some wine?"

"Tea would be great," Jay said, glancing at Hillie.

"For me, too. Thanks!"

Christina disappeared into the back room and returned with a tray holding a pitcher and two large goblets.

"Here you go." She sat across from them. "To get us started, I want you to know… I am the back office person. I'm the front office person. I'm the label designer. I'm the event planner and the sound system technician. I'm the wedding coordinator. We run on a very small bunch of people here. One of the best benefits of anybody coming into our environment is you'll come in the first time and not know where to sit or stand, but by the time you leave, you'll feel like family."

"I already feel that way," Hillie said. She sipped tea. Delicious with a hint of lemon.

"Let me tell you how we usually work with wedding couples," Christina went on. "Almost everyone who comes here is busy. This is the 21st century, and everyone is stressed out. Even if you could plan your own wedding, you don't have time. Am I right on that?"

Hillie nodded. "That's why we're here. I'm a set designer in L.A. so I could plan the event for sure. But when?"

"Wow. A set designer. I bet you've got some great ideas about what you'd like for the wedding," Christina said.

"A few ideas… but they aren't really solidified yet. We've been so busy looking for a place to have it."

"What's the date you're looking at?" Christina touched her pink iPad.

"June 15," Hillie said.

Christina flipped through a few screens. "That's open. Great! One hurtle passed already." She set the iPad down. "From the day we get you on the calendar, I'm involved one hundred percent in all your planning. I do it for free. I come with the venue. If you let me guide you, I'll take the stress out of your planning. Two weeks before your wedding, I'll know exactly how it's going to go.

"If there's a problem or a glitch, you probably won't even know it because I'll take care of everything. Normally, there aren't that many issues, but if there is, I'll take care of it and not alert the bride and groom unless it has to do with a family member. You have enough on your mind, so leave those details to me."

"What details exactly?" Jay asked.

"Decorations, flowers, music, food, tables, chairs, and anything that goes with the reception—you name it. There is no additional charge to use our equipment. Everything in our facility is free for you and your guests. The only extra charges might be when you need something we don't have and that means renting it from an outside company. You will be charged by the DJ, florist, photographer, and for the cake, of course, but we will help set it all up for you."

"This feels just like Tuscany," Hillie said, gazing out the open doorway.

"It's Old World," Christina said. "We're on top of a hill with a 360-degree view of nothing but paradise. The vines emit so much positive energy. It's a place to get back to your center."

"A great place to do yoga!" Hillie said. She told Christina about her hot yoga class.

"I love that!" Christina said. She went on, "Another thing, we have no cell phone signal here, so everyone at your wedding has to be in the moment. It's a place where people are talking to people and not tweeting and not texting and not Facebooking."

Hillie looked over the materials in front of her. "Can Jay and I have a moment to talk privately?"

"Certainly. Take your time. Would you like to stroll outside for a few minutes? Go down by the vines. That's a great place to collect your thoughts." She stood. "When you're ready, just ring the bell and I'll come down."

They didn't say anything until reaching the lawn. Hillie stepped onto the grass, slipped out of her sandals, and closed her eyes. Jay stood behind her and wrapped his arms around her.

After a long moment, Hillie said, "What do you think now that you've seen it?"

"What's not to love?" he said. "It seems perfect, especially the part about Christina working with us for free."

"Yep," she sighed, content. "Let's do it."

Holding hands, they went down the stairs to give Christina the good news.

"Wonderful!" Christina hugged Hillie. "I always love working with Rabbi Sam's clients. The more connected the officiant is to the couple, the more memorable your wedding will be. With the ceremony twenty minutes long…"

"…twenty-two and a half," Hillie chimed in with a mischievous grin.

Christina's eyes twinkled as she laughed. "Exactly! The best weddings bring in the couple's life experiences, and Rabbi Sam is a genius at that. It should also be a learning experience because there are so many interfaith weddings now. Great ceremonies are funny and memorable. Everyone there will be talking about it for the next fifty years."

"That's got Rabbi Sam all over it," Jay said. He gave Hillie a short squeeze from the side. "Great work, honey. I'm starting to get excited about the wedding myself."

"Yay!" Hillie applauded. "That made my entire month!"

"Would you like to sit down and go over some things now?" Christina asked. "Or we can set up another time to get into the details."

"There are a couple things we could talk about now," Hillie said.

They moved back to the table, and Hillie pulled out her brown leather notebook.

"We only do one wedding per week," Christina said, finding some forms within the stacks on the table. "That means you get very personalized service every step of the way."

"Do you have a list of what you do as the wedding planner?" Hillie asked. "That might be the best place to begin."

Jay spoke up. "I'm seeing your caterer listed here. What about kosher food?"

Hillie spoke up. "Rabbi Sam said you have a kosher caterer available, right?"

Christina nodded. "Yes... We have two in the area. We have worked with Kosher style menus, but it can get expensive. It depends on how many guests will be Kosher." She pulled out two brochures. "We'll contract with the Kosher caterer, if you prefer, but the prices will be much more than what we charge for our gourmet chef."

Jay nodded.

Hillie felt a pang. Now that they were down to actual figures, money anxiety was starting to hit her.

They talked with Christina a few more minutes, then headed to the car. As Jay drove onto the freeway, Hillie said, "You know something crazy? Now you're getting excited about the wedding, and I'm thinking more about going to Vegas!"

He darted a look at her. "Why?"

"The cost!" she said. "Wow."

"We're actually pretty conservative in what we're spending, right? Some places charge fifty or a hundred grand just for the venue."

"I know. I guess this just started getting real."

What a Wedding Planner Does

Full Service planning involves everything included in the wedding: managing the budget, vendors, venues, and Day-Of Coordination.

Budget

Before considering any venues or making appointments with any vendors, everyone must agree on the total budget for the wedding. They wedding planner watches the budget and stays in communication with the wedding couple, so there are no surprises.

Venues

Comparing venues and offering options to the wedding couple, along with verifying available dates saves the wedding couple time. Venues are often booked over a year in advance. Booking the venue will often be the single greatest expenditure for most couples and even small differences in fine print can cost thousands of dollars.

Vendors

A list of recommended vendors saves the wedding couple time and frustration. A wedding planner works with certain vendors over time and can vouch for the talent and dedication of these vital service providers.

- Photographers
- Videographers
- Florists
- Caterers
- DJ or Band
- Bakery
- Bartender
- Printer

If the wedding couple does not require help with all of these details, the wedding planner will have checklists and resources to help them stay on track in a timely and cost-effective fashion.

Day-Of Coordination

The wedding planner also acts as the Day-Of Coordinator, taking care of all the logistical details on the day of the wedding.

Timelines:
- Wedding Day agenda
- Photographer
- DJ or band
- Wedding Planner's own timeline

The wedding planner creates detailed timelines for the entire duration of the wedding. The wedding couple, their families, the photographer and DJ should approve the timelines to ensure everyone is on board. Everyone in the wedding party receives a copy at the rehearsal, as well.

Rehearsal
The Day-Of Coordinator ensures that everyone in the wedding party and everyone who will be escorted into the ceremony attends the rehearsal, if possible. The Day-Of Coordinator supervises the rehearsal, which usually takes place one or two days before the wedding.

Wedding Day
On the day of the wedding, the Day-Of Coordinator supervises all vendor setup and answers any questions

that arise. They cue the wedding couple, DJ or band, and photographer for each event (grand entrance, first dance, cake cutting, etc.). The Day-Of Coordinator is the go-to person for the vendors, so the wedding couple can enjoy their special day.

Distributing the personal flowers and ensuring everyone is in place, the Day-Of Coordinator ensures each participant is fulfilling their responsibilities and that guests are treated properly. Once it is time for the ceremony to begin, the Day-Of Coordinator signals to begin the music and keeps the processional flowing as planned.

After the ceremony, the wedding planner ensures the guests quickly move to the reception venue while the wedding party is at their appropriate place for photos.

Wrapping up

After everyone is gone, the wedding planner makes sure all of the client's personal property and wedding gifts are properly packed and secured, and that rented items are returned on time.

Chapter 7

The Wedding Planner

Man is not king of his castle, until his wife puts the crown on the top of his head.

~ The Book of Proverbs

Hillie stopped in for an early hot yoga class the following Thursday. Currently between set projects, she pulled a personal day to get some planning done for the wedding before her afternoon appointment with Christina.

Amanda met up with Hillie outside the open classroom door. She had her phone in one hand and a clipboard in the other. Amanda had been away for more than a month on an extended vacation.

"Hey!" Hillie said. "Welcome back!" She dropped her tote bag for a hug as other class members swept past them.

At that moment, Sally Wilson paused for a quick hello. "Monday night girl's night out, right?" she asked.

"I'll call you," Hillie promised. "We've got to talk about the wedding!"

Sally touched her arm. "Not tonight! I have a date." She laughed and went into the classroom.

"How are wedding plans coming along?" Amanda asked.

"We've decided on the rabbi and the venue. Major steps."

Amanda's eyes lit up. "Details!"

"Rabbi Sam, of course. And Gershon Bachus Vintners."

"Isn't he great?" Another hug. "Temecula Valley is so beautiful. The pictures you're going to have!"

"You know of Gershon Bachus?"

She laughed. "Of course. Rabbi Sam told us about it. Kosher-style wine, right?"

Hillie chuckled. "You got it." She told about having Christina as their wedding planner.

"That's the smart way to go. I did my own wedding and it was beyond overwhelming... practically impossible. I was too exhausted to enjoy the first few days of our honeymoon." Her phone chirped. She glanced at it and back to Hillie. "How about the in-laws?"

The spark went out of Hillie. She quirked in the corner of her mouth. "I wish I could give you good news on that... but..."

Amanda's phone chirped again. "Let's get together. When Ross and I got married, we went through that, too." She flicked her thumb across the screen on her phone. "Do you have your calendar? Let's get a lunch date set up."

They agreed to meet the following day, and Amanda scurried away, her blond ponytail waving with every step.

Back at her apartment, Hillie pulled out Christina's checklists along with her notebook and some additional checklists from the Internet. She put Miles Davis on Spotify and started a fresh pot of coffee.

Four hours later, she glanced at the time. Any later and she'd hit rush hour traffic. Quickly, she packed up her paperwork and her laptop and headed for her car. As she hit Interstate 15 South, she felt a surge of excitement. Finally some concrete plans for the wedding. She couldn't wait.

Hillie was still thirty minutes out from Temecula when Jay arrived at his parents' brick rancher in Long Beach, their home since Jay was in grade school. A long red waste container stood near the end of the driveway. They were in the last stages of a remodeling project that had lasted for almost three years.

His sister Joy was in from Fairfield for the week, so this would be his chance to talk about wedding plans with everyone in the family at once—including sampling Rabbi Sam's bottle of wine.

When Olivia opened the door, Jay stepped inside and kissed her cheek. "Whoa." He glanced over her head. "Look at those floors." Red oak hardwood gleamed where tired green wall-to-wall carpet had been.

"They finished it last week." She sniffed, annoyed. "The smell in here…"

"It'll fade, my dear," Max said, striding toward them. "Looks great, doesn't it, son? Lights up the whole house."

"I noticed it right away, Dad." Jay handed the bottle of kosher-style wine to Olivia. "Take a look," he said, as she took it. "Kosher-style wine from Temecula Valley."

Olivia lifted her glasses from the top of her head and put them on to read the label, her mouth pinched in concentration.

"We're having the wedding at this winery," Jay told her. He closed the door behind him and slipped out of his shoes, a habit as deeply engrained as bringing wine when invited for dinner.

"What's that?" Max asked, moving closer.

Olivia showed him the bottle. "He says it's kosher-style wine made in Temecula. We get our wine from Israel."

"Which winery?" Max asked, taking the bottle for a closer look.

"Gershon Bachus Vintners. We're having kosher food and kosher-style wine right there at the winery. It's a beautiful location."

At that moment, Jay's four-year-old nieces—identical twins Cloe and Zoe—bolted down the hall, giggling. They wore matching shirts from the latest animated movie. Cloe's was pink and Zoe's was blue. They grabbed Jay's legs, looking up at him, their dark eyes dancing. "Uncle Jay! Uncle Jay!"

Joy hurried after them. "Girls! Let your uncle breathe." Laughing, she leaned forward to hug Jay over their heads. Her curly hair was an exact match to Jay's except Joy's reached halfway to her waist. She had clear eyes and an open expression. Her husband, Reuben, was an airman currently deployed in Afghanistan.

"Good to see you!" Jay said. "How's Reub?"

She backed up a little to give the girls room to move. "I talked to him this morning. Seventy-two more days…"

Jay bent down to hug the girls as best he could. Milky skin with liquid brown eyes—the only way to tell them apart was Cloe had bangs and Zoe didn't. Before he could say anything more to them, they dashed off down the hall.

Joy smiled as they disappeared. "They're watching old family movies."

Max shifted the bottle in his hands. "I had my thirty-five millimeters put on DVD and colorized."

"That's really, really old," Jay said. "It's a wonder they're interested."

"They think I'm you, Jay, and you're wearing funny clothes," Max said, laughing. "That's was when I still had hair."

"Dad!" Joy said. "You have hair. You cut it off."

He reached up to affectionately brush his gray flat-top back and forth—a style he had worn for more than thirty years.

While Jay and Joy chatted, catching up, they all moved to the dining room. The table gleamed with the daily china—white with gold rims—and a white linen tablecloth.

A stack of silverware sat on the corner. Joy picked it up to finish setting the table.

Olivia told Max. "Let's try out the wine tonight. I've got to get my lasagna out of the oven." She hurried into the kitchen with Max following her to get the corkscrew.

Joy moved closer to Jay. "How's the wedding coming along?" she murmured.

"The wedding's coming along fine," he whispered, frustration in his voice. "It's the family that's…"

She nodded. "It was bad enough for me, and we're both Jewish. I can't imagine the headache you're going through."

"We want to do the right thing," he blurted out. "Hillie has been so great about it, trying so hard to honor our traditions. But she's not getting any credit for it."

"And she won't," Joy said. "I'm sorry to say it, but she won't."

The doorbell rang.

"That's Tamara," she went on. "Would you let her in? I've got to help Mother get set up."

Jay trudged to the door. Beautiful enough to be model material, Tamara was their youngest sibling—twenty-seven years old with wisdom far beyond her parents and grandparents and anyone else who might be around. She was on her way to being a famous singer— at least that's what her latest agent kept promising. At the moment, she sang backup for a startup cover band still struggling to fill their calendar. By day she worked as a receptionist in a dentist's office.

If Jay were brutally honest—which he didn't have the heart to be—he would have advised her to keep her day job.

When Jay opened the door, Tamara's almond-shaped eyes narrowed. "So, the troublemaker has the nerve to show his face." She wore ankle-high black boots and dark stockings with a black leather skirt that stopped just above her knee. Her nails alone would have paid for an evening of fine dining.

She reached up to kiss his cheek.

"Hi, Tamara," he said, slightly bored. "We're in the dining room."

She stopped to pull off her boots, replacing them with soft socks dug from her black leather handbag. "What's the temperature like inside?"

"Chilly with a chance of storms," he said, reverting back to their teenage jargon. "I brought a peace offering, so maybe…"

She patted his back regretfully. "Silly boy." Leaving her handbag on the narrow table next to the door, she made an entrance into the dining room. Jay slowly trailed after her.

When everyone was settled around the table, Max picked up his wine glass in a salute, and they all did the same. Jay watched his mother's face as she sipped, paused, and shared a look with Max.

"That's good," she said, savoring and sipping again.

"It's delicious!" Max said, turning to Jay. "This is made in Temecula?"

"Less than two hours away." Jay chose a piece of garlic bread from the cloth-lined basket and handed the basket across to Joy. The twins sat on each side of her, signaling to each other across her middle. She shushed them.

"So, tell us about the wedding plans," his father said.

Suddenly, Jay felt all eyes on him. He told them about the winery and the wedding planner, the outdoor patio and the great photo ops.

The discussion turned to photographers. Jay mentioned to Olivia that photographers in Temecula seemed very reasonably priced, as opposed to other areas. Olivia approved.

Olivia's lasagna had been a family tradition since Jay was a little boy. He dug in, savoring the meal as one listens to the quiet in the eye of a storm, knowing the second squall was about to hit.

"What about the wedding party?" Olivia asked. "Who is going to stand up with you?"

Jay touched his linen napkin to his mouth. "We haven't gotten that far yet."

Olivia went on, "Your sisters should be in the wedding."

"I'm not sure what Hillie has planned. Neither of us is solid on that yet."

"You should have six girls and six men," she went on. "The twins can be flower girls and Joy should be the Matron of Honor."

"Mom," Joy protested, "Hillie chooses who her Matron of Honor will be. She'll want her best friend."

Before she could answer, Tamara said, "What about the music? I could sing…"

"You should let your sister sing." Olivia continued without waiting for him to answer—not that he had an answer. "That's the one thing you can do for your family. Tamara should sing. She's a professional. It would be disrespectful to leave her out."

Jay's throat clamped down. He gulped wine and stretched his neck. "I'm sure that will be fine, Mom…" He glanced at his sister sitting next to him. "I'll call you, sis."

She glowed.

Jay had a sudden compulsion to roll his head back and rake his face with both hands. He fought it down and forced a smile in Tamara's direction. He managed to hold off the face clawing until he got to the car.

Hillie arrived at her appointment with Christina a few minutes before five. This would be a late night for Hillie with work in the morning, but she didn't care. Progress fed her soul.

Christina met her at the door of the winery. "Need help carrying something?" she asked, noting Hillie's file box and briefcase.

Hillie handed her the file box. "I brought everything. Most of my notes and samples are real, not virtual, so I lugged them along."

Christina hefted the box and headed for the same table in the tasting room they had used before. "This is exciting!"

"Better than my thirteenth birthday party," Hillie said. "And that was pretty great."

Christina set down the file box. "Iced tea?"

"Water would be great," Hillie said, opening her briefcase.

A glass ice-water dispenser sat on a barrel nearby. Christina picked up a paper cup from the stack and filled it for Hillie. "Let's see what you've got."

Hillie pulled out her paperwork. "There are so many things to cover. Where do you usually begin?"

"Let's talk about the style or theme you'd like for your wedding. Give me some background on where your inspiration is coming from or maybe a wedding you saw that you'd like to use as a springboard..."

Hillie ticked them off on her fingers. "Three things are shaping my concept: Jewish traditions, our story (Jay's and mine), and my mother. She and I used to play a Wedding Game when I was a girl."

"Tell me about the Wedding Game."

Hillie related the story of the paper dolls and how that led to a game where she created her Dream Wedding with her mother. She pulled out her parents' wedding album. "I also want to include some elements of my parents' wedding as a tribute to my mother."

"Is your mother still with us?" Christina asked.

Hillie softly shook her head. "She died in a car accident when I was fifteen."

"I'm so sorry!" Tears filled Christina's eyes. "My mother passed away a few years ago. It must have been hard to lose her at that young age."

Hillie nodded, then looked up, blinking.

Christina retrieved a box of tissues from a nearby side table. "Look at us." She let out an ironic chuckle. "And we're just getting started."

"It was bound to come up," Hillie said pressing her eyes with a tissue. "My mother is an integral part of the wedding. I have her wedding dress, and I'm going to see if I can have it altered." She opened the wedding album and showed it to Christina. "That's the dress. I tried it on and it's in good shape. With some adaptations, I think it could work."

"How beautiful! That's a timeless style." She looked closer. "Are you thinking of matching her bouquet?"

"I hadn't thought of matching the flowers. I guess it depends on how difficult that would be." She reached out to turn a couple of pages. "See how the ribbons swoop across the altar of the church? I was thinking maybe we could do something like that."

"Is it okay if I make copies of some of these?"

"Sure."

They looked at a few more photos, then Christina said, "If you could name one emotion you'd like your guests to get from the wedding, what would that be?"

Hillie considered. "Peace and harmony."

Christina laughed. "That's two, but we'll go with it. How do you feel about blue?"

Hillie picked up her blue moon necklace and held it out for Christina to see. "This is my favorite color. I was born on the rare blue moon in '88, so that's kind of been a lifelong theme for me."

"My son was born in May '88." Christina smiled and added, "It's a lovely necklace. We can do a lot with that."

They talked for almost two hours, creating to-do lists for both of them.

"Oh, before I forget, I'm supposed to pick up two bottles of kosher-style wine while I'm here."

"White or red?"

"White. It's for dinner with Jay's family."

"Let me get that for you now while we're thinking about it," Christina said and disappeared into the back room. She set the wine on a nearby table, and they returned to their conversation.

"The officiant makes all the difference," Christina said. "If the officiant is dry and boring, the wedding comes off as dry and boring. I love Rabbi Sam's ceremonies. He makes people laugh, and sometimes they cry. He keeps thing short and to the point, but he also focuses on making the wedding personal by including your story, taking time to honor passed loved ones…" She broke off, thinking. "I don't want to intrude on your day, but I just had an idea."

"What is it?" Hillie asked, anticipation in her voice.

"I wrote a poem about my mother. If you'd like Rabbi Sam to read some of it during your ceremony, you're welcome to use it. If you don't, that's fine, but you might want to take a look at it…"

"Of course!" As Christina scrolled through the files on her iPad, Hillie said, "Better pass out tissues before the ceremony."

"I know, right?"

A Tribute to Mother by Christina

A tribute to mothers
Should not be on just one day
Daughters wear their emotions freely
But may not take time to say

A few simple words of gratitude
Or a light touch on the arm
Instead a wall of resistance
That causes nothing but harm

The daughter grows up
And begins to spread her wings
Feeling confident and independent
Collecting experiences among other things

She graduates from school
With a masters and great GPA
Her mom stands in the audience
With smiles and words of praise

The pair share a moment
The celebration happy and grand
Mom standing against the bar
Watching daughter sing in the band

The next day they pack in silence
Only two in the room
Mom filling each box
Knowing they must leave to soon

Only a few days at home
The girl would again have to go
Her job takes her away
She feared what she did not know

They spoke every few days
But her job took so much time
There was not a whole lot to say
Mom was always last in line

She moved a few times over the years
Met a nice man to share her life
They discussed having children
She imagined being a wife

Only then did she sit back
And think about mom with a smile
Memories were overwhelming
Remembering mom's grace and style

She called home to say hello
Sat outside where no one could hear
She asked if she could come visit
In a few words mom said "yes dear"

The next trip was filled with laughter
They looked through albums on the floor
It had been a great week
And the daughter yearned for more

The girl spoke freely this trip
And told her mother she had a gift
She touched her mom's face softly
And mom was suddenly miffed

She told her mother of the fiancé
But that was not the surprise
She continued and stated her intent
To come home to be his bride

But that was not the best news that day
She continued to say there's more
They walked up to her old room
And opened up a hidden drawer

In the back was a book
It was her journal from teenage years
Verses from the years of silence
When mom's thoughts filled with fear

It was the girl's journal
She handed it to her mom
She asked her to open the pages
She sat down and touched the girls palm

With the girls nod the mom opened
The first two pages were blank
But on the third page was lengthy
Mom's eyes teared and heart sank

The opening line said "Dear Mom,
This is a tribute to you
I am writing them here
To show I know what you do

I did not find my voice
To share my days good or bad
But I found my days were better
Because I knew what I had

The mom looks up at her daughter
Now smiling from ear to ear
The daughter smiled back and said
There is something you now need to hear

You never knew that I admired you
You never knew I watched you each day
I knew that you felt disconnected
But for me there was no other way
I knew I would find my own rhythm
To manage my days and my nights
That I'd eventually talk more often
It was my own personal fight

But now I am here with you
Feeling closer than if we were twins
Because this week I knew
You would understand my sins

Now we can be friends
Sharing this next part of our lives
In the same place where you raised me
And having our family ties

We are coming back to live here
In this town near you
Jack will relocate
His family is around here too

We want the next generation
To benefit from your love
My life was filled with guidance and understanding
This was your gift to me.

Chapter 8

The Wedding Party

On the back of the groom's chair: Mr. Right.
On the back of the bride's chair: Mrs. Always Right!

After work on Friday, Hillie drove to Jay's one-bedroom apartment. They hadn't found a moment to talk, so they had a lot of ground to cover catching up. His kitchen was the size of a photo booth, stuck in the corner of the main room. Hillie had tried to cook there once and got so frustrated she refused to cook there ever again. Whenever they ate at Jay's, they had takeout.

They planned to spend most of the weekend getting his things organized and packing whatever he didn't absolutely need for daily life. Once the holidays set in, he'd have no time to get ready for his move into their rental house.

Usually fairly neat for a guy's place, things looked a bit disheveled with empty shelves and stacks of boxes slowly taking over the living room. His framed art stood against the far wall, encased in bubble wrap. Anything not in use was fair game for wrapping, stuffing and stacking.

When they got settled on his futon, Jay said, "You first. What happened at Gershon Bachus?"

"Christina is perfect," Hillie said. She told him about their conversation and how comfortable Christina made her feel. "She even gave me a poem about her mother that we can use if we want to. I want to include a tribute to my mother, and the poem actually made me cry."

Jay got up to answer the door and bring in the pizza and buffalo wings. He set the box on the coffee table and opened the lid.

"What about you?" Hillie asked, lifting a large slice of peppers and onions with extra cheese.

Jay grimaced. "I wish my story was as exciting," he said.

"Didn't your mother like the kosher-style wine?"

"She loved it," he said. "But she also has ideas about my sisters being in the wedding, and..."he paused for effect, "Tamara singing!"

"What?" Hillie's head tilted left.

"I wish it wasn't so." He let out an anguished sigh. "And that's not all. She's got opinions on everything." He rubbed his temple.

"What Rabbi Sam said is coming true," Hillie said. "I don't want to offend your mother, Jay, you know that..."

"BUT," he finished for her, "it's OUR wedding." He put his arm around her. "Who do you want in the wedding party?"

"Amanda," she said, counting on the fingers of her free hand. "Sally, my cousin Laney, and maybe Becca from work..."

"So, you're thinking four girls?" he asked.

She nodded, taking another bite.

"Could we possibly add Joy and Tamara to make six?"

She dabbed her mouth with a napkin. "Do you have six guys to fill in the other side?"

"Aghhh…" He sagged against the back of the sofa. "I'll have to scrape bottom to find six guys."

"See what I mean?" She leaned into him for a tomato-y kiss. "Eat some pizza, Jock. We've got to make some lists. You'll need your strength."

They spent the next hour cataloging their friends and sorting through Jay's male friends to identify who could possibly be in the wedding party.

"You know what we have here?" Hillie asked, grabbing the next-to-last piece of pizza. "The start of our guest list."

"At least all this won't be wasted."

Hillie laughed. "We haven't even started yet. Don't wimp out on me now."

By the end of the evening they came up with two lists. Besides the girls she had already mentioned, Hillie added some girls from her crew at work as back up in case her first-choice girls had to opt out.

For the men, Jay put down Brian Taub as Best Man, then Ron and Don. He figured they were certain to be in the wedding, then he filled in with some guys from his office and Hillie's cousin Vic for good measure.

By 7:30, they were on their cell phones calling everyone for confirmation—Hillie in the living room and Jay in the bedroom.

Half an hour later, Jay peeked out the bedroom door. "Are you on the phone?"

"Just hung up," Hillie said, stretching. "Amanda is great with being Matron of Honor. She is so amazing."

"Is that all you've called so far?" he asked, joining her on the futon.

"Sally's in, too," she said. "What about you?"

"I got through the whole list." He chuckled. "Ron and Don both asked me the same thing: 'Open bar, right?'"

Hillie laughed. "What else can you expect from Ronald McDonald?" her pet name for Ron and Don—two clowns who always appeared together.

"Brian's good. And the rest of the guys are from my office. I've got plenty. No need to touch base with your cousin Vic."

She threw her list on the coffee table next to the pizza carton. "I'll get with the rest of my girls over the weekend. I'm setting up a get together for the bridesmaids to discuss their apparel and other things."

Jay glanced at his watch. "If we leave now we can just make it for the late movie." He slanted his head, teasing, "Denzel Washington…"

She reached for her purse. "Buy me popcorn, and I'll follow you anywhere."

The following afternoon, Hillie was still at Jay's apartment. They had been working in his closet for the past two hours, sorting what to pack, what to donate, and selecting a few things to hang back up for wearing until he moved.

When they got started that morning, she had pulled on a ragged black shirt from his recycling pile, figuring she'd save herself some laundry and throw it back on the pile at the end of the day. It had a tear under the arm and a bleach stain near the bottom. But once she put it on, she realized the shirt felt soft and broken in. She liked it. Maybe she'd keep it to use for painting or deep cleaning.

Her phone rang. She flicked her thumb across the screen. "Hi Dad!"

"Sweetie, how are you?"

She found a small open space on the edge of the bed and sat. "We're packing Jay's apartment."

"Busy weekend, huh?"

"Always. This wedding stuff is exhausting. Was it the same for you and Mom?" she asked.

"Absolutely. I wanted to elope, but she wouldn't let me."

Hillie giggled. "That's what Jay keeps saying, too."

"All grooms do." His chuckle sounded deep in his chest. "I called with an invitation. Would you and Jay have time to come for Thanksgiving dinner?"

"I'm not sure," she said. "I don't know what his family has planned. Let me check with him and text you, okay?"

"Sure, honey."

"What do you have in mind?" Hillie asked.

"Dot's a fabulous cook. She's offered to make dinner for us at my place if you and Jay can come over."

"Sounds great." Hillie tried to sound excited. She should be excited. *What was wrong with her?*

"We can move it to Friday evening or Saturday after Thanksgiving if Jay's family has you locked in," he said. "We're flexible, so just let me know."

"I will, Dad. And thanks." She ended the call and sat staring at Jay's empty DVD rack in the corner.

"You okay?" Jay asked, coming out of the closet with a load of dress shirts in his arms.

She told him about the invitation.

"If he's okay with having it on Saturday, that would be perfect," Jay said. "We can hit both places and keep everybody happy." He looked closer. "You're not okay, are you?" It wasn't a question.

"I should be happy for him," she said, her voice quiet. "I'm such a terrible daughter."

He dropped the shirts on top of a mound on the bed, and knelt in front of her for a hug. "It's tough adjusting to family changes, and this is a big one for you."

"I'm twenty-nine years old! Not twelve."

"You're still Daddy's little girl, Hillie." He kissed her cheek. "You always will be."

She sighed. "It will be good to go there for dinner. I want to spend time with Dad and Dot, so it starts feeling normal and not such a big deal."

"You're an amazing woman," Jay said, squeezing her close. "That's not flattery, Hillie. I'm 100% serious. When I think about how much you deal with every day between your job, and putting up with me, then add in the wedding and now your father… You are amazing."

She pulled back to gaze into his eyes. "You see me, Jay. That's so incredible."

He stood and pulled her up into his arms. "Everything is going to even out in a few months. We're going to be okay."

On Thanksgiving Day, Jay and Hillie arrived at the Jaworski home shortly after 2:00 in the afternoon. Tamara met them at the door. She wore jeans and a pink tee-shirt with strips cut out of the back in a chevron pattern.

She took the Gershon Bachus wine from Jay. "Mom will be happy to see this," she said. She leaned in to whisper, "Happier to see the wine than to see you, I'm afraid."

"Now, sis," he said. "Let us at least get in the door before you rain on us."

Tamara smirked at him and headed back inside.

Hillie drew in a long breath.

The doorbell rang before they stepped away. Jay pulled it open, and the twins darted inside. They wore matching blue jumpers. Skirting around Jay and Hillie, they headed for the den.

"Cloe! Zoe!" Joy dashed after them. At a slower pace, in came an athletic young man with a military haircut and a few days of dark stubble on his chin.

"Reuben!" Jay exclaimed. He grabbed his brother-in-law into a hug. "When did you get back?"

"Last weekend. They let me go a few days early because of the holidays."

Joy headed back toward them, her cheeks flushed. "He surprised me." She playfully smacked her husband's side. "He actually rang the doorbell."

Reuben grinned. "I made her promise not to tell the folks."

"Come in! Come in!" Olivia called from the dining room. "Don't stand at the door all afternoon."

With his lifted palm signaling them to stay behind him, Reuben led the way into the dining room. Olivia shrieked and something glass crashed.

Joy said, "I'm not sure that was a good idea."

Jay chuckled. He pulled her into a sideways hug. "I'm so happy for you, honey."

Hillie followed them, a sinking feeling in her stomach. Holidays with the family were usually festive—a little icy from Olivia's corner, but Hillie always looked forward to seeing Max, and the twins were adorable. Maybe Reuben's return from Afghanistan would take attention off the wedding.

And it did… until dessert.

While serving cherry pie and non-dairy whipped topping, Olivia said, "Jay, tell us about your wedding plans. What's happening now?"

Jay passed a dessert plate to Hillie. "Not much has happened since the last time I was here, Mom."

Tamara spoke up. "We're going to have a meeting to talk about the bridesmaids dresses."

"Blue. They have to be blue," Olivia announced.

Hillie felt heat rising to her face. Jay squeezed her hand under the table.

"One thing I did want to tell you," Jay said. "Close to the winery there are homes that rent out by the night. The family can stay in one of those, so it won't cost so much for hotels."

"Private homes?" Max asked. He picked up the wine bottle to top off everyone's glass.

Jay nodded. "People rent homes to wedding families. There are so many weddings in that area, it's a common thing."

"Kosher?" Olivia asked.

"We can find out," Jay said. "The owners of Gershon Bachus are Jewish. It's possible we could find one."

Joy spoke up. "We can order in vegan, Mom. It could work."

Olivia nodded, considering.

Jay plunged ahead while he felt the advantage. "Having a home would make it easier—and cheaper—to host the Rehearsal Dinner, right Mom? We were also wondering if you'd like to do a brunch on the day after the wedding for anyone who is still in town… If you want to, that is."

Olivia's thin hand held the pie lifter in mid-air, her chin tilted. She slowly nodded. "We all have to eat," she said.

"Thanks, Mom," Jay said, smiling at her. He dug into his pie.

Hillie took small bites.

After surviving the Jaworski dinner, having a meal with Larry and Dot didn't seem so daunting. On Saturday, Hillie and Jay navigated through fairly light traffic and arrived right on time. Larry Gordon lived in a small Cape Cod in an older neighborhood north of Los Angeles. He had purchased the home ten years ago, after Hillie moved out, but she still had a bedroom there and a key. She never knocked on her father's door. He would have been distressed if she had.

Larry was putting a CD into his old player when they stepped into the living room. It still had the original dark paneling. Brilliant sunlight shone through sliding glass doors that led to the back patio.

A white Bichon dog darted out of the kitchen, barking.

Hillie froze. She had never seen that dog in her life.

"Hi!" Larry boomed. He dropped pushed a button on the machine.

Avoiding the tiny barking fur ball, Hillie dropped her tote bag on a chair and rushed toward her Dad for a big hug. He gave the best hugs in the universe.

Dot came out of the kitchen wearing a white apron covered with tiny red polka dots. "Trixie! Stop!"

The dog sat down. Her brown eyes glistened, two pools in the center of her white bristly face. Jay knelt to say hello. She sniffed his hand, then sat back to look at him.

"Can I?" he asked Dot, reaching for Trixie.

"Sure," she said, smiling. She touched his shoulder in greeting, then moved to Hillie.

Jay settled Trixie into the crook of his elbow. Guitar music filled the room. Simon and Garfunkel crooned, *Hello darkness, my old friend…*

"It's good to see you!" Dot hugged Hillie. "I made a pot roast. You're probably turkey-d out by now."

"A little," Hillie said. Dot made it easy to smile. "Can I help with anything?"

The ladies moved into the kitchen. "I've got potatoes on. They need a few more minutes." Dot glanced over the yellow Formica countertop—another house original. "You can serve the salad into bowls, if you don't mind."

Hillie got busy. Not that there was much to do. The table was set to perfection with cloth napkins folded on the plates. Hillie glanced around at the gleaming sink and the shiny microwave. Even the tile floor had a new glow.

Now that she thought about it, so did Dad.

"How are things going?" Dot asked. She was wearing pearl earrings in the kitchen.

"We're finishing up a project on the set," Hillie said. "Then our crew is off duty until after Christmas. I have a new project to plan, but at least it's a quiet phase. We won't get into production until January."

"Yours has to be near the top of the list of stressful jobs," Dot said, picking up two oven mitts.

Hillie chuckled. "Right up there with bridge builders and SWAT teams."

"I guess there's a difference between stress and stress," Dot said. She opened the oven door. A blast of heat made her draw back for a moment. "Our office is as quiet as a church, but we have our share of stress, too."

"I'd rather have my stress than yours," Hillie said. "I'd dry up and die doing what Dad does." She paused as Dot set the roasting pan on top of the stove. "What is your job at the office?"

"I'm VP of Operations. Luckily for us, Larry is in a different department. If I were his boss, things could get tricky."

Hillie drew up short. *Go Dad.*

Dinner was great. They laughed and ate, then ate and laughed. As things were winding down, Dot asked, "More cobbler?"

Groans sounded all around.

Hillie said, "That was a fabulous meal, Dot. I wish I could eat more. It was so good!"

Dot laughed. "I'll send some home with you." She stood and reached for plates.

Larry touched her arm. "Sit down, honey. We'll get the dishes. You've been in the kitchen all day."

Hillie started stacking plates, and Jay got the serving bowls.

"I'll put the food away," Dot said. "I want to make up some take-home containers."

Larry got up to help. He still tipped the scales at two-hundred pounds, but somehow he looked years younger. With all four of them in the kitchen, they kept bumping into each other while also trying to avoid stepping on Trixie. After dodging Hillie twice, Jay finally grabbed Hillie and started dancing with her.

"Okay, you win," Dot said. "It's too crowded. I'll sit this one out." She picked up Trixie and parked on a barstool. "Anything new to tell about the wedding?"

Inwardly, Hillie groaned. She was tired of repeating the same thing again and again.

Jay took over the report and talked nonstop for the next five minutes while Hillie cleared the counters and the stove.

When he came up for air, Hillie said, "Dot, do you know anything about signing up for bridal registries? I've got to get that done before much longer."

She nodded. "My daughter got married last year, and I went with her to register for a couple of stores. They give you a scanning gun, and you go shopping. Whatever you scan goes into their computer. It's pretty cool. Time consuming but cool."

"You have a daughter?" Hillie asked. She moved closer. "I'd love to meet her."

"Margo is a medical resident at UCLA. She sits for her M.D. boards next summer."

Suddenly, Dot had Jay's attention, too. He paused his pot scrubbing to ask, "What's her specialty?"

"Ob-Gyn," Dot said. "Last year she married Marty Parker, a guy she's known since Hebrew school. They live in Long Beach." She picked up her phone from the counter. "I have their wedding picture on here." She found the photo and handed the device to Hillie. Jay grabbed a towel and came to look as well. Larry closed the dishwasher door and joined them.

When Hillie saw the wedding picture, she caught her breath. Margo was every bit as beautiful as her mother, olive skinned and delicate with expressive brown eyes. She stood under a Chuppah beside a fair-haired young man wearing a white garment and yarmulke, similar to what Dan had worn in the Gershon Bachus wedding she had attended.

"They're Jewish," Hillie said, looking at Dot.

"Of course." Dot smiled softly at the image as she took her phone back. "I'm Jewish. My late husband was Christian. We each observed our own faith, except I didn't keep kosher. My parents didn't keep kosher either.

"Growing up, Margo went to temple with me and to church with her Dad. She went to Hebrew school and Sunday School. When she was old enough, she made her choice to have a bat mitzvah, and she has been observant ever since. She and Marty keep kosher at home."

Larry said, "You should meet Margo, Hillie. You would get along famously."

Hillie found her breath. "I would love that. Maybe over the holidays?"

Dot's smile lit up the room. "We'll work it out."

Dad pulled out a deck of cards, and they played partner Rummy until almost dark. First the two couples squared off, then men against the women.

When Dot lay down the winning points for the second time, Jay leaned far back in his chair, flexing his shoulders. "We'd best get on the road, don't you think, babe?" he said.

Hillie nodded. "I'm getting tired." She finished the last bit of her iced tea and gathered up the empty glasses on the table.

Larry said, "Next time, pack a bag and stay the weekend."

Hillie grinned and headed for the kitchen, calling over her shoulder. "So you guys can stay up half the night playing video games?"

Jay called out, "She's on to us, Larry."

"Seriously," Larry said. "Let's do that over Christmas."

"I can check with Margo and Marty," Dot said. "Maybe they can join us one evening."

Hillie and Jay gathered their few belongings and paused near the front door.

Hillie leaned close to Dot and murmured, "Is it okay if I call you once in a while?"

"Absolutely. I would love that." Dot reached for her phone, and they shared numbers.

Hillie closed her eyes for a moment in a silent expression of gratitude. "I can't tell you what that means to me. Between my friend Amanda and you, I might just survive this wedding after all."

Chapter 9

The Dress

A happy wife makes a happy life.

~ Proverb

Two weeks later, Hillie took her mother's wedding dress to Raquel, the manager of a local tailor shop her company used for outsourcing special projects. If Hillie trusted anyone to work on the dress, it would be Raquel.

For a business dealing with glamorous clients in the movie industry, the shop had little glamour itself. Tucked in the middle of a strip mall with a crumbling parking lot, it could have been a dry cleaner—a low counter across the entire width of the front room and nothing behind it but a bare paneled partition.

In the far corner, Raquel sat at a black sewing machine with gold lettering on it. Reading glasses rested on the bump halfway down her long nose. Her graying hair clung to her head in a boyish style. She was working on something with silver sequins covering it.

The moment Hillie came through the door with her long box, Raquel dropped what she was doing. "Hillie! What have you got for me today?" she asked. She had a Hispanic accent.

"Something special, Raquel," Hillie said, sliding the box across the counter. "This is my mother's wedding dress."

The older woman's eyes widened. "You don't say." She reverently raised the lid.

"I want to see if you can alter it for me, so I can wear it for my wedding. You're the only person I trust," she finished.

"How beautiful!" Raquel murmured, lifting the garment and turned it in the light. "It looks in good shape."

"It needs to be taken in."

"And modified a little?" Raquel asked, caressing the silk. Her bony hands had big knuckles. "Do you have time to try it on now?"

At Hillie's nod, she lifted a hinged section of the counter for Hillie to pass through.

Raquel returned the dress to its box and led the way into the back room where three women sat at sewing machines. Two of them smiled at Hillie and nodded. Across the room, a commercial ironing press stood next to an ironing board with a silver iron standing on it. The room smelled of starch and steam.

Without pausing, Raquel spoke to the stout one on the left. "Constance, watch the front for me while I work with Miss Hillie." She didn't wait for a reply. Hillie followed her into the fitting room where a clothes rack covered the entire back wall.

For the next half hour, Hillie stood on a low stool while Raquel tucked and pinned.

"This lace has seen its better days," Raquel said, touching the shoulder straps. "Would you like to replace it or remove it? In about five minutes, we could turn this into a strapless gown, very stylish."

"That would be perfect," Hillie said. "I'm going to wear this moonstone necklace." She touched the stone. "A strapless dress would make it stand out."

"These lace appliqués are creased, and some of the beading is missing. It will be easier for me to replace them than try to fix them."

"Can you match them?" Hillie asked.

She nodded. "Close enough so no one knows the difference. I will take care of it for you."

When they finished, Hillie changed back into her street clothes and brought the gown to Raquel. "How much will this cost?" she asked.

Raquel shook her head. "For you, nothing. Count it as my wedding present to you."

"What? I want to pay you, Raquel. I know how busy you are. And you're going to have to buy some things."

"You bring me good business," she replied. "You're easy to work with, and that's so rare." She shook her head, decided. "No. Let me do this it for you, muñeca."

Hillie hugged her. "Thank you, Raquel. I didn't expect anything like that."

"That's why you're a good person, Hillie," she said. "You don't expect it. This is my joy, to fix the dress so it's beautiful for your Wedding Day." She carefully folded the gown over her arm. "I'll call when it's ready for you to try it on."

With more thanks, Hillie returned to her car. She texted Jay as soon as she closed the door. *The dress is a go! I'm so excited.*

A few seconds later, he replied, *Awesome on the dress. My dad just called. Our presence is expected on the first night of Chanukah.*

Surprisingly, the holidays came and went with little drama. Caught up in Chanukah preparations, Olivia seemed to forget about the wedding, and they had an enjoyable time with the Jaworski family.

Over the Christmas-to-New-Year week, Hillie and Jay spent three days with Dad and Dot, including a visit from Margo and Marty.

Watching Dot and Margo together, Hillie felt a little squeeze in her heart. Mother and daughter looked so much alike, they seemed almost like older and younger versions of the same person. They laughed spontaneously and took delight in the smallest things. Hillie imagined that would be the way she and her own mother would have been. If Mom were still here.

Another heart squeeze.

She drew in a breath and focused on the conversation over their sushi lunch.

"We went to Vancouver for our honeymoon," Margo was saying. "It rained the entire time."

Marty picked up a dab of wasabi paste with his chopsticks. "I wasn't complaining."

His wife elbowed him in the side.

"I asked Margo to bring her wedding album," Dot told Hillie. "Maybe you can get some ideas."

"Great!" Hillie said, though the last thing she felt like talking about was the wedding. The holidays had given some relief from the constant pressure she felt these days.

After lunch, the guys moved to the living room to discuss Fantasy Football. Jay's league had just finished up with Brian Taub winning the pool the third year in a row. It turned out that Marty also belonged to a league.

Margo handed her wedding album to Hillie. It had a padded cover in some type of white leatherette material. Twelve inches square, it had an oval insert containing the same wedding picture Dot had showed them on her phone.

"This is nice," Hillie said, turning the book over for a better look. She sat at the table to open it.

"I found the album on Etsy," Margo said, pulling out the chair next to Hillie. She sat with one leg under her. "A woman in Kentucky hand makes them."

Dot joined them. "We spent most of the budget on a kosher reception, so we had to get creative with other things in the wedding."

"Did you do the Bedeken?" Hillie asked, glancing at Margo.

"Marty was terrified he'd pull off my veil while he was covering me, so I had the veil made with the top section shorter. It barely covered my face." She reached out to turn pages in the album. "See?"

"Was the rabbi okay with that?" Hillie asked. The style was unusual but still beautiful.

Margo leaned back laughing, completely pleased with herself. "We didn't have a dress check before the ceremony. Once I showed up wearing it, no one said anything. All Marty had to do was flip it over. It worked great."

"So you had a kosher caterer for your reception?" Hillie said. "We're dealing with that, too. Jay's family keeps kosher."

"The cost was out of sight," Dot said, "and the food could have been better."

Margo nodded. "It was pretty awful, actually."

"In what way?" Hillie said.

"Dry, bland…" Dot said, shaking her head. "We would have done better to go vegan."

Hillie stopped. "That gives me an idea. Jay and I love a vegan Chinese restaurant in L.A. They have fake meat that's delicious."

"Now you're thinking, girl," Margo said. She leaned over until her shoulder bumped Hillie's.

Suddenly Hillie had that coming-home feeling. The grieving little girl inside her stopped crying for a moment and looked up in wonder.

The next weekend, the bridesmaids met at Hillie's place for lunch. Hillie had already picked out the dress, shoes, and accessories. Getting the girls together was more about them get acquainted and finding out who could help with some of the wedding preparations—such as making favors.

Jay's sister, Joy, would be attending via Skype since she lived so far away in Fairfield.

Amanda brought a bottle of red wine. Sally brought white wine. Becca and Cara from Hillie's crew brought one of each. Hillie had a tray of sandwich makings and a giant salad on her dining table ready for when they took a break.

When everyone was sipping wine, Hillie connected with Joy on Skype. She set her computer to screen sharing, so Joy could see the pictures Hillie was about to show everyone. She set the laptop on the coffee table where the girls could see it from the sofa.

At that point the doorbell rang. "That must be Tamara," Hillie said.

Holding a wine glass and laughing, Amanda pulled the door open. Her expression stiffened.

Hillie looked up from the laptop to see Tamara come in. Two seconds later, Olivia came through the door, flushed from three flights of stairs.

For a moment, Hillie thought her throat was closing up. This was the first time she had been with Olivia without Jay acting as a buffer. Her mind went into damage control mode—and came up blank.

Amanda was pouring the newcomers wine and chatting with them. Hillie got up to welcome them, then she excused herself and closed herself in the bathroom to text Jay. *Your mother's here! She came with Tamara.*

Taking a few deep breaths, she returned to the living room. Her plans for a lighthearted happy celebration with the girls just turned into something far different.

"Okay, everyone set?" she asked, cheerfully. She felt like she was watching herself from a corner of the ceiling. "Let's start with the dresses."

Amanda said, "Can you email me the link? I have my iPad."

"Sure." Hillie's fingers flew over the keys.

"Got it," Amanda said. She shifted her chair, so Tamara and Olivia could see her screen.

"My theme color is blue to match my moonstone," she said, lifting the stone from her necklace. "As most of you know, before my mother passed, she gave me this on my thirteenth birthday. This deep blue will be the color of the bridesmaid dresses."

Olivia nodded at Tamara. So far so good.

"We're going with a very simple basic style." The dress had a high empire waist with tiny cap sleeves and a straight skirt to the floor.

Olivia pulled a small pad of paper from her purse along with a pencil. She adjusted her glasses and made notes.

Hillie went on, "Matching blue sandals with a kitten heel." She scrolled down. "And a simple strand of pearls." She looked around. "Does everyone have pearls?"

"I can borrow some," Cara said.

"Awesome." Hillie clicked the keys. "Amanda, I'm sending you another link."

"Got it."

Olivia bent closer to Amanda's iPad. "Earrings," she said.

Hillie nodded. "I'm afraid these will have to be purchased so everyone matches. All of this is on a web page. I'll email everyone the link after we're done here.

Olivia scribbled on her pad, then turned it around so everyone could see the giant numbers. "This is the cost," she said. "That's too much! Joy can't afford that much money. Can you afford that much, Tamara?" she demanded. "On a receptionist salary?"

A shocked hush fell over the room.

Hillie clamped her teeth to keep back some choice words that were aching to come out.

"Mom!" Tamara said. "The bridesmaids in Joy's wedding paid more than this. What are you talking about?"

That launched a full out argument between Tamara and her mother.

From Skype, Joy said, "What's happening?"

Hillie turned the laptop around, so Joy could see the dispute. Within seconds, Olivia's cellphone chirped, then Tamara's. Joy got them into a three-way call, and the argument went virtual since Joy's side of the conversation was also coming through Skype.

The other women in the room stared, mesmerized. Sally swiped her cellphone open and held it.

"You spent more than anyone in the family has ever spent on a wedding!" That was Olivia to Joy.

"You're ruining everything! Get your purse and go home!" That was Joy to Olivia.

Hillie caught Amanda's eye and nodded toward the bedroom. They eased out of the room, but they could have done cartwheels for all anyone would have noticed.

"What are we going to do?" Hillie asked. She realized she was trembling.

"I don't know what we can do," Amanda said. "You want to call the police on your future mother-in-law?"

"It's not what I want to do, but what I can get away with," she retorted. She looked at her phone. Thirty minutes ago, Jay had texted her back. *I'm on my way.*

"Maybe we can separate them," Amanda said. "I'll see what I can do."

Hillie paused in the kitchen to drink a small glass of water. That helped settle her nerves a little. But only a little.

At that moment, the doorbell rang. Amanda opened it.

Jay dashed inside. His curly hair stood on end. "What's going on?" he demanded, looking directly into his mother's eyes. "What are you doing here?"

"I came with Tamara," she said, her mouth was so tight it's a wonder she could speak. Little streaks of red lipstick filled the cracks around her thin lips.

Jay looked sternly at both of them. "Is this the way you act in someone else's home? Shouting at each other like two… like two…" He searched for a word.

"…meshugganahs, Jay! That's what they are. Meshugganahs," Joy yelled out over Skype. She went on as though she were standing in the room, "I'm so embarrassed, Mom. How will any of us show our faces again?"

No one spoke for a few seconds. Olivia touched her purse hanging from her arm, as though to remind herself it was there. She glanced at Tamara and marched toward the door. Tamara hugged Jay, waved apologetically at Hillie, and followed her mother out.

The moment the door closed behind them, Hillie's legs went weak. She sat in the closest chair.

"Are they gone?" Joy asked. Sally turned the laptop to answer her. After their brief conversation, Joy said, pleading, "Hillie, I'm so sorry. I don't know what got into Mother. I'm so sorry."

Jay took the laptop. "It's not your fault, honey," he said. "I'm here now, and everything's okay."

"I'm going to sign off now," she said. "I've got to take a nerve pill. Please tell Hillie how sorry I am."

Jay nodded and closed the laptop.

"I wish she were here to pass those pills around," Amanda joked. She stood and reached for the nearest wine bottle. "I don't know about the rest of you, but I'm having another glass of wine before I say another word."

Relieved chuckles filled the room, and wine filled their glasses. "To weddings!" Amanda said, clinking all around.

Cara picked up her purse.

"Please stay," Hillie said, reaching out to Cara. "There are more things we need to discuss. It's not fair to waste the entire evening for everyone." She turned to Jay. "Do you mind hanging out for a few minutes?"

He reached for a roll to build a sandwich. "I'm on call tonight, so I might have to dash out, but I'll hang around for a while."

Hillie sat next to Amanda who had their list of items to talk about on her iPad.

They discussed making favors, exchanged contact information so the girls could stay in touch about a bridal shower and the dozens of other things girls talk discuss at times like this.

After Jay and Hillie saw the last girl to the door, Hillie turned to him. "What a fiasco! What an absolute disaster! We were supposed to have a girl party. It was supposed to be FUN."

"I'm sorry, Hillie," he said.

"Sorry? You think sorry is going to fix this? Those girls are my friends. Two of them are on my work crew." She groaned. "Think of the gossip! I'll never hear the end of it."

She squared off with Jay. "That's it, Jay! I've tried to be nice and go along with whatever your family wants, but this is the end of it." Her hand sliced through the air. "Your mother insisted your sisters be in the wedding in the first place. Now she wants to tell me how much the dresses should cost to accommodate them? Can't you see how ridiculous that is?"

She bore in on him. "She created the situation, and then she makes it miserable for everyone involved, including you."

His eyes flashed. "What do you want me to do? I broke every speed limit trying to get her to help you. Can't you see I'm doing everything I can?"

"Everything you can?" She drew in a short breath, and let it out in a gasp. "You're the biggest pleaser I've ever seen. You bend yourself into a pretzel trying to keep everyone happy. And now you're bending me into a pretzel, too."

He tried to touch her. She brushed his hand away. "Is this what our life together is going to be? Pleasing your mother day after day after day? Your mother who CAN'T be pleased!"

Her voice grew plaintive, imitating Olivia's voice. "'You have to come for dinner. You have to come for first night of Chanukah. You have to… You have to…'" She scowled. "Well, I don't have to, Jay. Do you hear me? I don't have to."

"Sweetheart, listen to me," Jay said, his voice calm. He stared into her eyes. "Listen to me. Let's get quiet, okay? Let's not say things we'll regret later."

"Who is going to regret?" she demanded. "This has been building up, and I have to get it off my chest. I need to know, Jay. How much of this pleasing stuff are we going to do after we're married?"

He pulled in his lower lip, a sad expression on his face. "Hillie, you are my first priority. Always. That's my commitment to you. If you feel miserable going to family dinners, you don't have to go."

"What about if we have kids?"

He hesitated, eyebrows together. "Would you keep our children from their grandparents?"

"No. That's not what I mean." She shook her head. "What about sending our kids to Hebrew school because your mother says so?"

His expression cleared. "That's not going to happen. We will agree on what our children do. You and I and no one else. Okay?"

Tears seeping out, she sank onto the sofa. "I've had too much wine," she said. "I feel sick."

"After this awful night, you can have another glass as far as I'm concerned." Jay sat close to her but didn't touch her. "My sisters and I are horrified at how things went tonight. You know that, right?"

She nodded. "What are we going to do? I don't know how NOT to get into disagreements with your mother. Olivia is cruel to me! Jay I want more from you!"

"I'm going to have a talk with my dad," he said. "Not that he can do anything much either. I don't know what the answer is. I want to protect you from all this, Hillie. Honestly I do. It's driving me crazy."

She moved closer to lean her cheek on his shoulder. "We need to talk to Rabbi Sam. He said this would happen, but I had no idea how bad it would be."

Jay put his arm around her.

She went on, "I haven't spent that much money yet. We can still cancel the wedding and not lose too much on deposits."

He picked up her left hand and kissed her diamond. "You still want to marry me, right?"

"Of course." She kissed his cheek. Her voice sounded sleepy. "Las Vegas here we come!"

He shifted to face her and pulled her closer. "Come here."

Chapter 10

The Priority

A woman understands a man and loves him.
A man loves a woman and but never understands her.
~ Rabbi Marc Rubenstein

L ate the next morning, Hillie was finishing her second cup of coffee and trying to muster enough energy for the day when Amanda called.

"I wanted to touch base," Amanda said. "We didn't get a chance to talk after the party last night."

"After the fiasco last night, you mean," Hillie retorted. She put her phone on speaker and placed her empty cup in the dishwasher. "Jay felt so bad about it that I felt bad for him. I guess that's the word for this whole situation, bad." Her socks sinking into the carpet, Hillie reached the sofa and stretched out with her head resting on the arm. She balanced the phone near her ear and closed her eyes. "I have a headache. Too much wine."

"How well I remember the whole wedding drama thing, honey," Amanda said. "It can get rough. For some reason family members seem to think they have some kind of ownership in every wedding that comes along. Everyone has that happen. It goes with the territory, I'm afraid."

"I never expected Olivia to be so aggressive," Hillie said. "Coming to my house uninvited… Making a sign to show everyone?" She sighed.

"My family thought I wasn't spending enough," Amanda said. "It's a no-win situation."

Hillie murmured, "It was like living in a nightmare. Surreal."

"The worst thing was you didn't see it coming. In one split second everything shifted, and you felt blindsided."

"I left a message for Rabbi Sam. We're going to set up a meeting with him sometime next week." Hillie covered her eyes with both hands. "It's too much. Jay is moving into the rental house this week. He just left to pick up more boxes. We're supposed to go over to his place and finish packing today. By the time we're finished, he going to be living out of a carry-on bag."

"Can he stay at your place for a couple of days?"

"It's too far from his office. Especially during rush hour." She wiped her eyes and sniffed. She felt like she was coming down with something.

"I know you don't feel like talking right now, but when you come into the studio for your class next week, stop at my office. We need to talk about my Matron of Honor duties and get things started there. I have some ideas that might smooth things out for you."

"Amanda, you are the greatest. Thank you."

"You've got it, sistah." She chuckled affectionately. "Drink a lot of water and take a nap while he's gone, okay?"

"Thank you, Amanda." She ended the call.

Hillie got up from the sofa, paused long enough to drink a full twelve ounces at the refrigerator door, and trudged to her room. Thank G-d for blackout curtains.

With an appointment set up with Rabbi Sam for later in the week, Hillie somehow got through the weekend. She almost skipped her Monday yoga class, but ended up going anyway. She had a three-year record to keep up.

On her way out, she stopped at Amanda's office and knocked on the open door frame.

Amanda was digging deep into the back of a low file drawer. Startled at the knock, she looked up, and her blond ponytail whipped around.

"Sorry," Hillie said. "Do you have time to talk to me now? I can come back on Wednesday, if that's better for you."

"Not at all," Amanda said, pulling out a thick file with both hands. "I'm just getting ready to send some stuff to my accountant. It's getting to be that time of year again, you know." She dropped the file to her desk with a distinct thud.

"Don't remind me," Hillie said with a smirk. "It's hard enough for me as an employee. I can't imagine what it's like owning a business."

"We're not going there!" Amanda waved Hillie to the chair in front of her desk. "Let's talk about something positive. The wedding!"

"Positive. Thanks for being optimistic." Sinking into the chair, Hillie pulled her leather journal from her bag. "Amanda, there's no way to properly thank you. You led me to Rabbi Sam—who is amazing, by the way—and he led me to Gershon Bachus and Christina. And now you're basically saving my life as well. You're the gift that keeps on giving."

"Aw…" Amanda got up for a hug.

"I'm sweaty," Hillie said, hugging her.

Amanda laughed. "Everyone is sweaty around here. That's kind of the point." She sat at her computer and flicked some keys. "We've got several items to talk about. I made a list here…" The printer came to life. A page appeared in the tray.

Taking the printout from Amanda, Hillie said, "The only thing I see missing is the spa day for the bridesmaids, the day before the wedding. I'm sorry to add something to the list, but could you set that up for me?"

"You're thinking mani-pedis and facials, right?" Amanda typed in a note.

"Yes. I actually have a coupon in my email." She found it on her phone. "There you go."

They talked about a bridal shower and other details for the next half hour.

Gathering up her things, Hillie said, "We're both taking personal days on Thursday and Friday to get Jay moved. Dad and Dot are coming over to help unpack."

"How do you like the new girlfriend?" Amanda asked.

Hillie slowly nodded. "You know what? I actually like her. And she has a daughter our age who married a Jewish man. They keep kosher."

"Really? Let's get together with them, Hillie. The six of us—you and Jay, Ross and me, and your new in-laws."

"In-laws? You mean step…" Hillie burst out laughing. "Whatever they are, they're great. We spent time with them over the holidays. Margo and Marty."

"Wow. Something else you didn't see coming, but in this case, cause for celebration." Amanda pulled up her calendar. "Let's get a couple of open dates lined out now. How about if you call Margo and see what we can coordinate?"

"Let's look at February and March," Hillie asked. "That far out, we'll surely get a hit."

On Thursday, Rabbi Sam joined Hillie and Jay at a small diner in the middle of the afternoon. Red booths with brown marbled tabletops on one side and revolving red stools all the way down the long counter on the other side—this place had been around since Moses. Hillie and Jay sat close together in the last booth at the back, their empty lunch plates stacked on the table in front of them. The dining room was deserted except for a white-haired man eating lemon meringue pie at the counter.

Jay stood to shake hands when the rabbi reached them. He wore a blue blazer with a dark blue pullover.

"Thanks for meeting us here," Hillie said, shaking Rabbi Sam's hand. She had on the barest of makeup, and her ponytail sagged. "Our rental house is three blocks away. We saw the moving truck off about two hours ago."

Sliding in beside Hillie, Jay said, "I cleared a space on the living room carpet, and we laid on it for about an hour…"

"…too exhausted to get up," she finished with an attempt at a smile.

Rabbi Sam nodded, considering. "So, what was important enough to interrupt this day, of all days?"

Jay looked at Hillie with an expression that told her she had the floor.

"We had a disaster happen at my place last week," she said. "We both took off a couple of days to get Jay moved in, so we thought this would be a chance to talk with you about it."

"What happened?"

The server arrived to take their plates. Rabbi Sam ordered coffee. When the server left, Hillie told the story of Olivia's crashing her bridesmaid party.

Rabbi Sam listened closely. "Jay, have you been in touch with any of your family members since then?"

"My sister, Joy." He glanced at Hillie, informing her as well. "Joy called me the next day to apologize. She was beyond mortified."

Rabbi Sam asked Hillie, "Do you have a relationship with Joy?"

She shrugged. "We see each other at family dinners. That's all."

"Reach out to her. She's exactly who you need right now. It sounds like she has a good heart."

"Joy's great," Jay said. "She lives all the way in Fairfield, so we only see her every couple of months."

"Make the effort," Rabbi Sam told Hillie. "Right now you're building a family structure you will live with for the rest of your life. Find a time to reach out to Joy."

Hillie nodded. "I'm sending myself a reminder to do that tomorrow." She typed into her phone.

Pulling a small notebook from his inside jacket pocket, Rabbi Sam laid it on the table. "Okay, moving on to damage control with your mother," he said, talking to Jay. "What do you see as her primary concerns?"

"From what she's saying, Jewish tradition and money." He told about Olivia's objection about the cost to the bridesmaids.

Rabbi Sam leaned back. "Just to put things into perspective for you, how much are the bridesmaids spending?"

Hillie named a figure.

"That's about half what I usually see, on the average." He shrugged. "You're doing good, Hillie. No need to change anything there. When someone agrees to be in the wedding party, they know they'll have to pay for their clothes." He made a small gesture with his flattened palm. "Enough on that topic. As for the traditions, we made up a list of things that will help Olivia feel better about the ceremony. You still have that, right?"

Hillie nodded. "It's in my leather journal."

"The wedding is still six months away. We will revisit that a little later. What I'd like to point out right now is this." He paused to look at each of them. "What have you been working on for the past four months?"

Hillie's chin came down, trying to understand what he was getting at. "The wedding."

Rabbi Sam said, "Bear with me. I'm going somewhere. What about the wedding?"

Jay said, in rhythm, "The venue, the wedding planner, the dresses, the food…"

"Exactly," Rabbi Sam said. "You've been focusing on The Big Day. What I'd like to talk with you about is your priorities. What is the most important part of the entire wedding day?"

"The ceremony," Hillie said. "That's why we're there in the first place."

"Exactly. They won't remember the flowers or the music or the fanfare. What everyone will talk about is what you say about each other and what I say about you."

Jay put his arm around Hillie and gave her a quick squeeze. She leaned her head against his cheek.

Rabbi Sam continued, "This is what we started out with. Remember? You contacted me, why?"

Hillie straightened up to answer. "I wanted to find a rabbi who would help us have a meaningful ceremony."

"My point exactly, Hillie. That's what I want to bring you back to. It's so easy to get lost in all these details and forget what's really important. Those 22½ minutes are like a spotlight on a dark stage.

Such a tiny space but without it, there's nothing." He waited for the server to set down his coffee, then went on, "You have Christina planning for you now, right? And a Matron of Honor?"

She nodded. "Amanda is taking care of a lot for me."

"Good. Let both of them work for you. That's what they are there for." He turned to Jay. "Your mother is going to come through this one way or the other. Before long, this wedding will be family history. We're going to do the very best we can, but once we do our best, the wedding is going to happen as it will. No one can control everything."

Jay drew a deep breath.

Rabbi Sam drummed his fingers on the table. "So, the ceremony…"

Hillie said, "I don't have my journal with me. It's back at my apartment."

"No worries," Rabbi Sam said. "This isn't going to be complicated. You're going to decide on three elements."

Jay pulled a couple of napkins from the metal holder on the table and reached for a pen in his pocket. Hillie typed into her phone.

Rabbi Sam ticked off on his fingers. "Your vows. Your story. Which traditions—Jewish or otherwise—you want to have in the ceremony."

"And honoring my mother," Hillie added. "How is that usually done?"

"You can use several means," Rabbi Sam said. "Sometimes we place an empty chair for that person. I've seen people set up a little display with flowers, a picture, and a candle on the seat of the chair. Sometimes there is a framed photo on the table with the Ketubah. You could also do something different, whatever you like. You'll also want to write something for me to say about your mother."

She nodded, typing with both thumbs. "Maybe Christina's poem…"

Rabbi Sam pulled out his own phone. "I'm going to send you a file folder with several examples of vows written by former clients. They gave me permission to share these." Scrolling, he said, "I have them in a draft folder in my email. Here we go... Okay, you should have that."

Hillie nodded.

He went on, "In the blue folder I gave you when we first met, you'll find some links for online resources if you need ideas. Once you've done your research, make sure you're writing vows that come from your heart. You are making promises to each other that will stay with you for the rest of your lives."

Jay asked, "Should we show them to each other?"

Rabbi Sam grinned. "Some do, and some don't. My advice is to write them when you're alone then read them together. You wouldn't believe some of the things I've heard, including foot rubs and promises to care for their dog children." He chuckled, then grew serious. "Your wedding ceremony is no time for surprises. You get one shot at this, so take time over your vows. Write them, let them sit for a month or two, then pull them out to look at them with fresh eyes."

Jay said, "Our story about escaping into Avila Adobe on our first date. That would be good." He was doodling on the napkin.

"And the hot air balloon going over Gershon Bachus," Hillie added.

"Do you want to write that?" Jay asked her.

"Tell you what," she said. "I'll tell the story into my phone recorder and send it to be transcribed."

"Great idea," Jay said, lighting up. "We can send it to Holly. She's a freelancer who does transcription for the office."

They high-fived each other, and all of them laughed. It felt good.

"Is there anything else you need at this moment?" Rabbi Sam asked.

"I haven't seen my mother since the night of the party," Jay said. "Any suggestions?"

"Hug her," Rabbi Sam said. "Don't say anything. Just hug her. It works miracles." He slid his phone into an inside pocket on his coat.

Jay held up the napkin he had been doodling on. It had stick figures that somewhat resembled a bride and groom holding up wine glasses in a toast. Across the top he had written in block letters G.L.A.S.S. and underneath Groom Likes A Simple Service.

Rabbi Sam laughed. "That's what you're getting, you know. A G.L.A.S.S. wedding by Rabbi Glassman."

Jay's chin pulled back. "I didn't think of that. Cool!"

Hillie took the napkin from him. "You have too much time on your hands, honey."

Chapter 11

The Vows

When a woman says she has nothing to wear
that means she's going shopping.
When a man says he has nothing to wear,
it's time to do the laundry.
~ Rabbi Marc Rubenstein

Hillie and Jay agreed to slow down their pace on the wedding plans for a couple of months. Rabbi Sam was right. Christina and Amanda were on the job, and they had a full six months until the Big Day. It was time to take a breath and focus on what mattered most: the ceremony.

Late in January, Hillie pulled up the resources Rabbi Sam had sent her. It was time to get some ideas for their wedding vows. Jay was on call this weekend, so she was spending a couple of lazy days at her apartment. She felt totally self-indulgent and more relaxed than she had for months.

Sitting cross-legged on her bed, she had her laptop open, a legal pad in her lap. At work she had two monitors, at home she had one monitor plus pen and ink for taking notes. She hated flipping back and forth between tabs on her browser.

Suddenly, she had an inspiration. She grabbed her cell phone and texted Jay, *Can you talk?*

Five seconds later, her phone chirped.

Jay said, "What is it, babe? That was perfect timing. I'm walking out of the hospital."

"How about this? We write our vows for the ceremony and also make them part of the Ketubah. Like an edited version of our vows mixed in with the Ketubah language. What do you think of that?"

"What brought that to mind?" he said.

She leaned back against the padded headboard. "I love the idea of having a framed Ketubah in our home. It's such a lovely keepsake from the wedding. I just thought that we could have a memory of our vows—in some form—within the Ketubah language. Sort of personalize it and make it our own."

"I don't see any problem with that. Rabbi Sam gives a framed Ketubah as his wedding gift to the couple, so he'll take care of the details for having it made." He hesitated. "That means we'll need to get the Ketubah wording to Rabbi Sam pretty soon, and I haven't even thought of writing my vows yet."

"Tell you what, I'm listing out some quotes that I'd like to consider having in my vows. How about if I make a list for you from my research? They are always together, the bride's and the groom's vows, so it would be easy for me to do that for you."

"Great idea, Hillie. I have some ideas of my own, of course, but that would help me get started. Right now I'm staring at a blank page and wondering what to do next."

She went on, "I've been looking at some sample vows he sent us. These are pretty short. Half a page or less."

He chuckled. "Hasn't anyone ever told you it's harder to write short than it is to write long?"

"Where did you get that from?"

"College composition class," he said. "Sorry for bringing up an unpleasant memory."

She let out a low laugh. "Too bad you can't come over tonight."

His voice softened. "Too bad is right."

They said good-bye, and she got off the bed to refill her coffee mug.

Back to her research, she started listing out quotes she liked:

"I receive your promise with love."

"I will stand with you as companion, lover, and friend."

"I will be strength, I will be light, and I will be hope."

"I will create with you a family home."

"I will be your best friend, life partner, and wife now and forever."

"I will trust you, respect you, and be faithful to you."

Beautiful language but pretty standard. Then she found something that made her pause. "What Steven admires about Monica" and "What Monica admires about Steven."

Excited she pulled the laptop closer, brought up a blank document and typed non-stop for the next ten minutes. She could write an entire book on what she admired about Jay. What a fabulous idea to take their ceremony up a notch.

She leaned back and closed her eyes to let things settle in. The service was starting to gel in her mind. She picked up her laptop and headed for her dining room table. Time for some serious typing.

The following Friday, Hillie drove to their rental house after work. Her commute would double from fifteen minutes to half an hour once she moved—but it was a temporary arrangement until they could buy a place of their own. They already had searches set up on a couple of real estate sites.

Bags and boxes of kitchen stuff filled her backseat—what she could spare from her place supplemented by a recent trip to IKEA. Coming from his bachelor pad, Jay didn't have enough cookware or appliances to make a single decent meal. That was about to change.

So was life as he knew it.

She was halfway there when she got his text, *Held up at work. Home around 8.*

A few minutes later, she pulled into a Vietnamese takeout place and got a large order of noodles. Jay could nuke them when he got home. No cooking for this gal tonight.

Saturday morning, Hillie set up the kitchen to her liking while Jay worked on his vows. Since he had no interest whatsoever in that area of the house, she had free reign. On the counter she had her color-coded diagrams, including the work triangle and prep stations.

Hillie and Jay were in the same area of the house since the open floor plan had the kitchen on one side of the great room with a breakfast nook in an alcove next to it. That's where Jay worked: at his tiny dining room table covered with papers and open medical books. Some things never change.

The rest of the room had no furniture except Jay's black futon, glass-topped coffee table and big-screen television.

Close to noon, she asked, "Ready for a break? I have grilled cheese on. It'll be done in about three minutes."

"Sounds great," he said, stretching. "Writing vows is even harder than I thought. It's not so much about saying enough. It's about not saying too much. I've been to weddings where everyone is asleep by the time they stop talking. I don't want to drone on and on."

"Except for the part where you're saying what you admire about me," Hillie teased. "Then you can definitely drone."

He got up to wrap her in his arms. "I can't believe we're this far along," he said, caressing his cheek against her hair. "Just a few more weeks, and you'll be moving in. Can you imagine that?"

She murmured deep in her throat, "I'm already here, Jock. I'm already here."

Suddenly, she lunged away. "Grilled cheese! It's burning."

He yelled, "That one's yours!"

She threw the wet sponge and left a damp mark on his shirt.

A few minutes later they retreated to the futon. Jay brought his laptop, so they could go over their vows together while they ate.

"This is so sweet, Jock. It touches my heart just reading it." She reached for his screen to advance the page with the back of her knuckle. Her fingers were buttery. "We can let this rest for now. Then come back in a couple of weeks to look at it again. Okay?"

He let out a relieved sigh. "So we can move on to something else?"

"We need to look at the order of the ceremony to decide what parts to have in it."

"I know. Flowers for the mothers, the music, the Seven Blessings..."

"Exactly." She got up to pull her journal from her tote bag. "It's almost like putting a puzzle together. We could be there for an hour if we put in everything."

"Same old story. Shorter is harder to do." He leaned over to look into her journal. "What have you got?"

They spent the next hour and a half going through the journal, deciding on what they wanted in the ceremony and what to leave out. Finally, they had a list.

Jay typed it into his laptop and sent it to Hillie via email. "So, what do you think?" he asked, closing the lid. "Should I run this by my parents?"

"By your mother, you mean?"

He stiffened.

"I'm sorry. I'm not being critical." She touched his sleeve. "Tell me why you want to take the ceremony to your parents."

"If Mom sees how much Jewish tradition we're putting into the ceremony, she might lay off me for a while," he said. He tapped the still-open page in her journal. "This is mostly Jewish, you know."

She nodded. "I love the meaning behind these. They say love and good wishes, and that's what the wedding is all about." She shrugged. "Sure. Go ahead. Would you like me to go with you?"

"Are you up for that?"

"I'm a big girl, Jay. I've stayed away from family dinners as much for you as for me. You feel so much pressure when I'm there, like you have to protect me. I'm going to be a part of your family, and it's going to be what it is.

"Besides, after what happened at the bridesmaid party, maybe it's a good idea for me to go with you and break the ice with Olivia. Let her see I don't hold a grudge."

His voice went to a lower pitch. "The thing is, Hillie, she does. She does hold a grudge. Can you deal with that?"

"Jay, she's your mother. As long as I don't have to move in with her or see her every week, I'll be okay."

He nodded, still unconvinced. "Next family dinner is a week from Thursday. I'll let them know you'll be with me."

She kissed him. "It's going to be all right."

What was I thinking? Hillie asked herself the following week as they got out of the car at the Jaworski home. She had sounded so brave in their living room, but now she had butterflies in her stomach and a sudden longing to spend the evening alone on her own sofa instead.

Jay put his arm around her waist. "We'll leave in two short hours," he said. "I set my phone to go off and changed my alarm to sound like my ringtone."

She pulled in a long breath. "It's going to be fine." *Who was she convincing, Jay or herself?*

Max opened the door as they reached the front step. He grinned at Hillie and pulled her into a fatherly hug. "It's so good to see you." He looked into her eyes, and she saw he meant it.

"Good to see you, too, Max."

"What, no wine?" he asked Jay with a friendly slap on the back.

"Fresh out of the good stuff," Jay replied. "Next time we're at Gershon Bachus we'll pick up some."

"They have a wine club," Hillie added. "It's online."

"I'll have to check that out," Max said, leading the way to the dining room.

Olivia had just set lasagna on the table. Jay hugged her. Hillie stood nearby.

Max reached for a chair. "Here you go, my dear," he said to Hillie. "Next to me."

She sat.

Olivia headed back to the kitchen, and Jay sat across from Hillie. They spent the better part of an hour in small talk and eating dinner.

"How is your father?" Max asked Hillie, handing her the bread basket for the third time. She set it aside.

"He's doing great," she said.

"Better than great," Jay added. "He's seeing someone. First time since her mother passed."

Max said, "You don't say! Is that a good thing, Hillie?"

She nodded. "I like her. She works at my dad's office. She lost her husband a few years ago."

"And she's Jewish," Jay added, smiling at Hillie.

"Born Jewish?" Olivia asked, looking directly at Hillie for the first time.

Hillie nodded. "Her daughter is married to a Jewish man, and they keep kosher."

"If that don't beat all," Max said. "Are they from around here? We should get together."

Jay said, "We'll have to see what we can work out." He pulled a folded paper from his shirt pocket. "Hillie and I have been working on our wedding ceremony." He handed the paper to his father. "We thought you might like to see what the service will be like."

Max unfolded the paper and scanned it. Before he could speak, Olivia took it from him.

Her lips tightened. "What about remembering your grandparents? And Uncle Jordy and Aunt Guta?"

"We can add them," Jay said. Hillie nodded.

"You're not going to do the Circling Seven Times?" Olivia said. "It's for protection."

Max said, "Olivia…"

She threw the paper to the table. "Something terrible will happen, Max. They have to have the protection."

Hillie had no idea what to say. Jay just sat there. *Why didn't he say something?*

"This whole thing is going to end bad," Olivia pronounced. "Very bad." She dropped her cloth napkin to the table and left the room.

After a long pause, Max said, "She has apple crumb pie for dessert. Does anyone want coffee to go with it?"

"Is it decaf?" Hillie asked.

"Yes. We always make decaf at night."

"That sounds wonderful," she told him.

When Max left the room, Hillie opened her mouth to ask Jay why he didn't speak up. He raised his hand, palm toward her, and she closed it again.

Later, he mouthed.

Olivia brought the pie to the table with a plastic bowl of whipped topping. Max followed her with the coffeepot, and their dinner went on as though nothing had happened.

More small talk. Hillie was about to explode with boredom and frustration. She hated small talk, and she never skirted around issues. If she had something on her mind, she said it and got it over with. This Jaworski family dance was getting tedious.

"We have a favor to ask, Mom," Jay said before they left.

Olivia waited, watching him.

"Would you mind picking out the place cards and candles for the tables at the reception? The winery has gold tablecloths, and the wedding color is blue, so anything with gold or blue would be fine with us."

"You have great taste, Mrs. Jaworski," Hillie said, trying to sound pleasant. "We'd appreciate your help."

Olivia glanced at Hillie. "You want me to pay for these?" she asked.

Jay stepped in. "We'll pay. We just thought you might like to pick them out. We'll send you the guest list to have the place cards printed."

"How many tables?"

"The tables hold eight, so we can plan on twenty," Hillie said.

"I'll go to Benjamin's Stationery next week. We always have our printing done with him."

"Thank you, Mother," Jay said. Feeling like a fifth grader, Hillie thanked her, too.

Shortly afterward, they said good-bye and headed to the driveway. The night was breezy and a little cool. Across the street, the neighbors had their garage door open and the light on.

When they got into Jay's car, Hillie said, "Why didn't you say something?"

"When?" He put his car in gear, and they moved into the street.

"When your mother said that about something bad happening because we aren't having the Circling Seven Times in the wedding."

He pulled into a nearby grocery store and found an empty space on the edge of the lot. Their faces were dim shadows from the streetlights overhead.

"We need to talk about this," he said. "It's something I haven't gone into with you yet, and this as good a time as any."

Her heart squeezed. "Are you mad at me?"

He looked at her, surprised. "Mad? Absolutely not." He reached for her hand. "I just need a few moments to focus on our conversation when I'm not driving. This is important."

She squeezed his hand and waited.

"My mother has a tendency to go off in a burst of heated words when she's worried or upset about something. When she gets like that, no one can say or do anything to bring her back to earth. The more we try to talk to her or reason with her, the worse she gets. I've seen her so upset that she'll go to her bed and howl for hours. The best I can tell, it's an anxiety problem."

"So, that's why you didn't say anything?"

He nodded. "It's also why my dad acted as though nothing was wrong. The more calm and centered we are, the quicker she will snap out of it."

"What if something's really wrong? How does she get anyone to listen to her?" Hillie asked, concerned. "Aren't you just shutting her out altogether?"

"That's Dad's territory," he said. "We children can't do anything about her emotional state. Believe me, Hillie." He touched her hand to his lips. "We've all tried to reason with her—all three of us—at one time or another. This is how we cope because nothing else seems to work."

"And that's why you went around me on the trip to Puerto Vallarta," she said. "You thought I might get into a spin."

"I'll never do that again," he said, ruefully. "I learned my lesson on that one."

"It makes me sad," Hillie said. "If my family had shut me out because they had me somehow labeled, I'd feel so alone."

"Like I said, that's Dad's department." He kissed her lips, then put the car in gear to back out of the parking space. "Let's get home. I want nothing more than a hot shower and a good night's sleep."

Chapter 12

The Ceremony

I have found the one that my soul delights.
~ Ketubah

For three weekends in February, Hillie and Jay worked hard at setting up their new home. They painted the powder room candy-apple red with glossy white trim—a nod to a 1950s set Hillie had done a few years before. Such bold color felt risky to her, but she liked the result. Brilliant white hand towels and the white mirror frame looked great against that color. Painting was as far as they could go with changes besides putting down a few area rugs. This was a rental after all.

In early March, Hillie was on a restaurant set deciding where to place the artwork when she got a phone call. Caller ID showed Raquel from the tailor shop.

She signaled to Becca to take over, and stepped aside, expecting to hear about the custom drapes she had ordered for the bedroom set.

"Hi, Raquel," Hillie said. "Tell me something good!"

Rachel's Hispanic accent came through. "Your dress is ready for a fitting. Bring your shoes."

"Great!" Hillie breathed, excitement rising. "We can talk about the veil while I'm there." They set up a time for the following week and ended the call.

Shoes. She had to find a pair. There went the weekend.

But as it turned out, she found just what she wanted online, paid a little extra for fast shipping and had her shoes in plenty of time. She found a white satin shoe with a low kitten heel. It had ribbons crossing the toe, held by a tiny rhinestone buckle on the side.

The moment Hillie stepped into the tailor shop, Raquel dropped the pink silk she was sewing. Her smile made her thin face glow. "You are going to love it, muñeca." She lifted the counter gate for Hillie to pass through. "I can't wait for you to see it."

In the dressing room, Raquel lifted the rustling white fabric over Hillie's head and guided it gently down around her. Before Hillie saw her image in the mirror, she already felt transported to another space. Her mother's arms cradled her. She closed her eyes for a moment.

A gasp brought her around. Raquel's three staff members stood nearby with enraptured expressions, looking over Raquel's work.

Hillie made her way to the low stool where three mirrors captured all sides—her creamy shoulders, the moonstone necklace, her slim waist and the appliqués across the organza overskirt. The lines fit her form as though sculptured. It took her breath away.

"I'm glad you have low heels," Raquel said, kneeling to look at the hem. "We have just enough room to get this exactly right." She pulled pins from the pincushion on her wrist. "I don't have to touch the whole hem. Just a little in the front."

"The stars were aligned," Hillie murmured. "My dad is going to freak when he sees me."

Raquel said, "And your groom…"

"Jay," she said. "Believe me, he's not going to see this until I'm walking down the aisle."

"He will cry," Raquel said, nodding. "He has to cry."

After the fitting, they spent an hour looking at veil styles in books and online. Hillie instantly knew which one she wanted when the picture came up—a Mantilla style that gave a nod to her Catholic heritage. It was so perfect she felt an ache in her middle.

When she left Raquel's studio, Hillie had a hard time returning to work. She would much rather curl up on her white bedspread and close her eyes to absorb all of this. The wedding of her dreams was really happening. And it was light years beyond what she'd hoped for.

She got back to the movie set as the last chair went into place for a poolside shoot. Only they were Adirondacks, and she had ordered loungers.

That night Jay arrived at Hillie's apartment in time for dinner. When he arrived, Hillie was lifting fettuccini from a boiling pot with a wide strainer and filling a serving bowl piled with bits of pulled chicken.

"Hey!" she called from the kitchen when he let himself in. "I'm in here!"

He gave her a peck. "I'm starved."

"Good. This is enough for two dinners and a couple of lunches. We'll be ready in about seven minutes."

"What can I do?" he asked, washing his hands.

"First the salad and then pour the wine." Moving quickly, Hillie stirred her homemade Alfredo sauce on the stove and tasted the wooden spoon. A little more black pepper.

He took salad from its grocery store wrapper and filled two bowls. Putting the remaining greens in the fridge, he asked, "Did you get with Margo to set up a dinner date?"

She nodded. "Amanda and Ross can't make it, but Joy and Reuben are available, so we'll still have six." She poured the sauce over the fettuccini and chicken. The heady aroma of garlic and cheese filled the air.

"That's awesome," he said, pulling his cellphone out of his pocket. "What's the date?"

"Just a sec," she dropped the saucepan into the sink and reached for her phone, so they could coordinate calendars. "Next Sunday," she said. "That okay?"

"Perfect. I'm not on call that weekend." He typed it in. "I'm glad you called Joy. You should know each other better. She's a wonderful person."

"I had a gut feeling I should call her," Hillie said. "I've learned to listen when that happens."

Jay poured Moscato while Hillie grabbed garlic bread from the oven.

He groaned. "This smells so good. It's killing me. I haven't eaten since six this morning. How much longer?"

"We're ready, Jock," she said, slanting a look at him. "You never were known for your patience. Hmmm? That time on the Santa Monica pier…?"

He gave a hoot. "*Under* the pier, you mean? On a warm night in August two years ago?"

She leaned in for a kiss. "You got it."

"I sure did," he said, smugly. He dished up Alfredo for both of them, and they ate in silence for a few minutes, enjoying the food and soaking in the peaceful moment after a hectic day.

"How did your fitting go today?" Jay finally asked.

"It was great," she said, twisting her fork into the pasta. "The dress looks incredible. Raquel has the magic touch."

"What's the next step?"

"A final fitting in about six weeks, then Raquel will deliver the dress to Gershon Bachus the week before the wedding—all pressed and ready."

"She's going to deliver it?"

Hillie nodded. "She's been one of my vendors since I first started on the job. She's doing the altering as a wedding gift, and she insisted that she deliver the dress herself. She wants to make sure it's exactly right." Hillie picked up her wine glass. "Raquel is amazing."

"You're amazing," Jay countered, lifting his glass to clink with hers. "You're the kind of person who attracts such loyalty." He grinned and his chin came down toward his chest. "Case in point."

She drew in a long breath and clinked his glass. "I love you, Jacob Jaworski."

He kissed her. "I know."

On Sunday, Hillie and Jay arrived at the vegan Chinese restaurant shortly after 7:00 for their dinner date with Margo and Marty along with Joy and Reuben. Both those couples kept kosher, so this was a great chance to introduce them to the best-kept secret in Santa Monica.

A double storefront, the restaurant had large windows fronting the sidewalk. However, looking inside was impossible since the glass had posters and placards covering every square inch as high as a man could reach. The door on the left was the entrance. Jay pulled it open and they entered a hallway that opened in front of the takeout counter.

When Hillie and Jay arrived, Margo and Marty were waiting inside. They looked so much alike, they could have been brother and sister—olive skinned, classic Jewish nose, dark hair.

After hugs and handshakes, Jay told the tiny black-haired hostess, "We need a table for six. Another couple is joining us."

"Name?" she asked, making a note. "Follow me, please." She led them to the front room on the other side of the wall to a round table in the corner. A long buffet table held a dozen warming pans, with salad and fruit on ice at the end of the line.

"We always get the buffet," Hillie said, after they ordered two pots of tea.

At that moment, Joy and Reuben arrived. She had her curly hair pulled up in a mass of tiny waves and ringlets with glittering drop earrings. Her face had a special glow tonight.

"Reub!" Jay said, shaking his brother-in-law's hand. "It's hard for me to get used to seeing you home."

"It's not hard for me to be home," Reuben said grinning. He held a chair for his wife with one hand. When she sat, he brushed his hand lightly on her shoulder for just an instant. She looked up and smiled at him.

Once they got settled and finished introductions, the six of them began sharing their vocations. The men were quick to zero in on their dedication to golf, Fantasy Football and the latest video game. Reuben offered a fifteen-second statement about being a career soldier just back from Afghanistan, and Marty told of his family-owned jewelry store started by his grandfather.

"My father and I are partners in the business," he said. "Dad runs the Los Angeles store, and I run the one in Long Beach."

Hillie said, "Let me see your ring, Margo."

Margo held out her hand to show a marquis diamond with three baguettes on each side. It gave out bursts of pink as she moved her hand. Murmurs went around the table. "Marty designed it," she said, proudly.

"I watched our shipments for a year before settling on that stone," he said. "It's just shy of two carats."

Margot held her hand closer, still moving her fingers to watch the light winking from it. "I still get mesmerized by it," she said, laughing lightly. She affectionately nudged her husband's arm next to her.

"It's gorgeous," Joy said. "See mine?"

They spent the next few moments gazing at rings. Finally, Jay said, "Hillie designs movie sets in Hollywood."

"Everyone already knows that," Hillie said, shaking her head slightly and pulling back.

"Tell them some of the movies you've done," he insisted. "They don't know that."

"I don't want to get boring," she said, waving her hand backward.

"We're not bored," Joy said, eagerly. "Tell us!"

Hillie named a few titles. "And right now I'm working on a new movie coming out next year called *Done* with Emily Blunt and Ewan McGregor."

Joy's eyes grew round. "Do you get to see the actors?"

"Not usually. We're out of there well before the shooting starts... unless something goes wrong. Once I had to go on a live set to oversee the switching out of a sofa, and Denzel Washington was sitting in a chair going over his lines with his diction coach."

"*The* Denzel Washington?" Margo said.

Hillie chuckled. "My favorite actor of all time," she said. "My next project is for one of his movies, as a matter of fact."

"We might as well stop talking now," Joy said, leaning back in her chair and looking around the table. "No one's going to top that."

Hillie laughed. "What do you do, Joy, when you're not in Mommy mode?"

Joy laughed. "I'm a Certified Tea Sommelier. Ever heard of that?"

Shaking heads all around. Reuben said, "It's like a wine sommelier but for tea."

"It's the top level of certification," Joy added. "So, basically I'm an expert in the culture, blending, and brewing of fine teas from around the globe." She glanced at Reuben. "That is, if I can keep up my certification requirements."

"You will," Reuben said, with a nod in her direction. He turned to the group. "She can travel around the world as a high-end tea buyer, or develop new tea flavors in a lab, or act as a consultant for quality assurance. Not to mention training more tea experts for certification."

"I'm already working for two places not far from where we live," she said. "If I have to go out, I get a sitter for the girls."

"That's fascinating," Margo said. "I've never met anyone who does that. How did you get started?"

The conversation flowed effortlessly, like they had all known each other for years. Hillie reveled in the moment. An untapped part of her felt a deep sense of satisfaction. This was her family, the one she chose and the one that chose her—a glimpse of her expanded life as Jay's wife. She wasn't only joining his family, they were developing their own extended family in a broader sense.

Most everyone at the table was on a second plate by the time the conversation turned toward Margo.

"I'm a doctor," she said, filling her fork with fake shrimp. She had delicate ears, shown off by her short hairstyle.

"I've been meaning to talk to you," Jay said. "I didn't want to talk shop while we were at Larry's place for the holidays."

"We won't talk shop here, either," Margo said, laughing. "No one else wants to hear it, right?" She looked around the table.

"That depends," Joy said. "What kind of doctor are you?"

"Ob-Gyn."

Joy's expression froze for an instant. She glanced at Reuben beside her before leaning forward. "That's a crazy coincidence," she said in a stage whisper, "because I just found out I'm pregnant."

A shocked silence.

Jay recovered first. "Congratulations!" he boomed, delighted. He got up to hug his sister. On his way back to his chair, he playfully punched Reuben's shoulder.

Reuben laughed, delight on every feature of his face.

"When are you due?" Margo asked.

"September 8th," Joy said. "We're hoping for a boy. *One* boy."

"Once you have a set of twins your chances go way up of having another set," Margo said.

Joy nodded. "Let's not even go there."

Jay picked up his water glass. "To the proud parents... for a healthy happy addition to their family."

Everyone toasted to that.

"We agreed to wait to tell everyone until the three month mark," Joy said. "I lost my first pregnancy and Mom went nutso for weeks."

Jay nodded. "She cried every day for a month."

"So, not only was I grieving about losing the baby, I was also guilty for making Mom feel so bad," Joy said. "Not going there again."

The talk moved on from there, and the evening ended before anyone was ready. It seemed like they couldn't talk fast enough to say everything they wanted to say.

As they were gathering their things, ready to go, Jay hugged his sister again. "I'm so happy for you." He gazed into her eyes, smiles bouncing back and forth between them. "When are you telling Mom and Dad?" he asked.

"We're going to visit them tomorrow."

Reuben put his arm around his wife. "We're staying at a hotel a little south of here tonight," he said. "My mom has the kids, so we decided to take advantage of it."

"I'm so happy for you!" Hillie said, hugging Joy. "Let's talk next week, okay?"

Hillie and Jay paused to thank their server before walking to their car, so they were the last to leave. When they were in private, Hillie said, "You know what this means, right?"

"What?" he asked, watching traffic in his rearview mirror, looking for a break so he could pull out.

"Joy's going to be six months pregnant for the wedding. She won't be able to wear the bridesmaid dress she just ordered."

Chapter 13

The Family

May the hand of G-d, the face of G-d, and the light of G-d
be upon both of you.
~ **Priestly Benediction**

Hillie called Jay's sister Joy the next morning to suggest Hillie make a visit to their home in Fairfield.

"It will be fun," Joy said. "Stay overnight. It's too far to drive all in one day."

Hillie took a personal day on a Wednesday near the end of March and drove to Fairfield after work the day before. Joy and Reuben lived in a modest housing development near the military base in a yellow split-level home with a two-car garage, complete with a small tree in the front yard—like every other house in the neighborhood.

Hillie arrived a little after 9:00 evening. When she reached the front porch, Joy stood at her open front door. She wore a white shirt and navy sleep pants with yellow emoticons all over it—smiling, winking, tongues out, crazy-eyed, all of them.

Behind Joy, the house was quiet with dim lighting. Opening the screen door, she spoke in hushed tones. "Let's get your things into the guestroom. Have you eaten dinner?" She had fatigue lines around her mouth.

"I stopped and picked up something to eat on the way," Hillie whispered.

"You'll be over the garage in the FROG," Joy said, leading the way up carpeted stairs next to the front door. "We use it for an office most of the time. You won't have to worry about noise up here. That's what I like about it. The girls can be running through the house screaming, and I can still concentrate."

"Did you say frog?" Hillie asked. She carried her tote bag and her purse, just enough for a short overnight.

"Family Room Over Garage," Joy said, over her shoulder. The stairs turned right and Joy opened a door at the top. They entered a large sage-green room with a bank of built-in shelves covering the entire back wall. Pushed together into an L, two tables filled the right front corner—complete with two monitors on one side and a large printer on the other.

A massive TV and sectional sofa claimed the left front corner. The sofa had a bed pulled out and made up.

"The bathroom is here," Joy said, opening a door and flicking on a light. "Would you like me to bring you a cup of tea? I know you're tired after a very long day."

"That sounds lovely," Hillie said. "If you don't mind, I'd like to get some sleep, and we can talk in the morning, okay?"

"That works. I'm tired, too."

Hillie set her tote bag on the nearby lounge chair. "How are you feeling?"

"I'm pretty much over the morning sickness," Joy said. "I just can't shake the constant exhaustion. From the time the girls get on the K4 bus until they get back, I'm either on the couch or totally sacked out in the bed. Reuben has been so great to help me get the house cleaned up for your visit. Can you imagine? Big dude wearing fatigues and folding little nighties?" She smiled and that glow came back for a moment.

"Maybe I should have waited…"

Joy patted Hillie's back. "Not at all, Hillie. I'm so glad you're here. It's way past time. I should have invited you up long ago. I'm so wrapped up with the girls…"

"I get it. There's no way I can even imagine what your life is like managing those two cute little balls of energy 24/7."

"Reuben is on swing shift, so he'll be in around midnight." Joy headed for the stairs. "I'll have the tea for you in about five minutes."

She was back in four minutes carrying a small tray holding a steaming mug, a small container of assorted sweetener packets, and a spoon placed neatly on a folded napkin. She set the tray on the desk.

"How did you do that so fast?" Hillie asked. "I barely got my shoes off.

"We have a hot water feature on our dairy sink," she said. "It's the perfect temperature for tea on tap. One of Reuben's Chanukah gifts a few years ago. I love it!"

Hillie hugged her. "Get some rest. I'll see you in the morning."

Joy nodded and headed to the stairs, then turned back. "The girls get on the bus at 8:00."

"I'll stay out of your way until they are gone," Hillie said. "I'll enjoy sleeping in a few minutes, believe me."

"Good night," Joy said, and silently closed the door behind her.

Hillie changed into soft sleep clothes and kicked back in the brown suede lounge chair to savor the most delicious tea she had ever tasted. She texted Jay to let him know she had arrived safely, then wished him good night and leaned back. The quiet felt lovely.

The next thing she knew, she came awake at two in the morning. She had fallen asleep in the chair with the empty mug in her lap. Moving to the bed, she didn't stir for five more hours.

A few minutes past eight, a gentle knock sounded on her door. Hillie opened to see Joy looking fresh and rested, though a little pale. She wore an oversized blue shirt and black yoga pants. Shoes seemed to be optional at her house.

"How was your night?" she asked, stepping inside. "Wow. Thanks for putting the sofa back together."

"It's the least I can do," Hillie said. "I slept like a rock, thanks. You're right. It's quiet up here."

"Ready for breakfast?" Joy led the way downstairs and toward the back of the house where Reuben sat at the table with an iPad.

The kitchen was divided into two mirror images—a sink, stove, refrigerator, and dishwasher on each side of the room—with a double oven on the dividing line.

Reuben said hello and stayed long enough to be polite, then went out for a run. Hillie helped herself to the cereal and juice on the table while Joy poured coffee and joined her.

Joy sat across from her. The bay window behind her showed the full width of their fenced back yard with a swing set and a kiddie pool. "So, what brought you all this way to see me?"

"I wanted to spend some time with you. As we're getting closer to the wedding, I'm starting to feel like we're gelling into a real family. Dinner with the six of us was so amazing. Wasn't it?"

Joy nodded. "It was a blast. We've been talking about having a barbeque and inviting everyone. I wish we lived closer."

"I have another friend I want to introduce you to—oh, you met her on Skype at the bridesmaid party—Amanda, my Matron of Honor. She's the owner of the yoga studio where I go, and my very dear friend." She told about Amanda's marrying Ross and converting to Judaism.

"She's been a lifesaver to me," Hillie finished. "And she's a hoot! You would love her."

"I'll meet her at the wedding," Joy said, nodding. "I can see what you mean. Four couples, about the same age…"

"Isn't it great? Since my mother died, it's been just my dad and me. And I don't see him that much since I got my job in L.A."

Joy buttered a muffin. "Hillie, what are we going to do about the wedding?" she said, opening the conversation Hillie had come for. "I'm not going to fit into that dress by June."

"Has it arrived yet?" Hillie asked.

She nodded. "I'll get it when we finish eating."

"I'd love to see it. I haven't seen any of the dresses yet. But you're talking about fitting into the dress, right?"

"Yeah. What are we going to do?"

"I want you in the wedding, Joy. It means a lot to both Jay and I."

Joy sighed. "I'm glad to hear you say that. With Mother's insisting on everything, Tamara and I have worried about that. We don't want to push ourselves in and ruin your wedding."

Hillie's head tilted. "Please don't say that. We want you. Both of you. I can't tell you how happy I am right now with the way everything is coming together. I had my dress fitting and it's so beautiful…," her voice quavered "…it's going to be more than I ever dreamed of, Joy."

Joy's eyes filled. She nodded and swallowed back tears. "I'm so emotional right now," she said, pressing her fingers to her top lip. "Hormones."

Hillie chuckled, sniffing. "What's my excuse, then?" She drank coffee and set the cup down. "As for the dress, I'd like to get my dressmaker on Skype while I'm here and see what she thinks, okay? Raquel is a magician with things like this."

"We can use my computer in the office."

They finished up, and Hillie returned to the FROG to pack her toothbrush while Joy put on the dress.

The deep blue made Joy look regal, and the fit was perfect. For now.

After a few minutes of coordination via phone and computer, Raquel's face appeared on Joy's monitor. Hillie made quick introductions and explained the situation.

Raquel had Joy turn this way and that in front of her webcam. "You'll be how far along by the wedding date?" Raquel asked.

"Six months."

Raquel nodded. "That empire waistline makes it perfect for converting to maternity. Here's what we can do. You'll need to buy a second dress in size 16W. I'll take the skirt from the big dress to make a maternity skirt for you. It will cost you more, but we can do it, and you'll look beautiful."

Joy said, "What if I find out I'm having another set of twins, and I turn into a blimp?"

Raquel smiled. "We'll have an extra fitting one week before the wedding, and I'll nip and tuck for you. When I deliver the wedding gown to the venue, I'll bring yours along, too."

"You are an angel, Raquel," Hillie said. "Thank you so much!"

When they closed the connection, Joy said, "This is a lot of trouble. Are you sure you want to go through all this?"

Hillie said, "That's the question you need to ask yourself. Do you want to go to the added expense of another dress plus the alterations?

You could end up paying triple, and your mother was worried about the expense to begin with."

"Mother won't know a thing about this," Joy declared. "This is between us."

"I'll leave that up to you." Hillie hesitated, then went on. "Can I ask you something?"

Joy waited for her to go on.

"Do you have any suggestions for how we can help Olivia feel more comfortable during the wedding?"

Joy shrugged. "Keep her busy. That's the only thing I can say. When she's busy she won't have time to fret."

Hillie counted on her fingers. "She's doing the Rehearsal Dinner on Saturday night and the Wedding Brunch on Monday for those who stay over after the wedding."

"We've already rented a house with a great kitchen," Joy said. "It's ten minutes from the winery."

"That's great! First I heard of it." Hillie continued her counting. "She's taking care of the place cards and candles, choosing the song for her dance with Jay, and making a list of pictures she wants the photographers to take."

"You're having more than one photographer?" Joy asked.

Hillie nodded. "A male and a female. Christina's idea. She's amazing, by the way."

"I saw pictures of the venue online. Beautiful location."

"We're having a vegan caterer bring in food, then Christina's chef is going to grill Ahi fish for those who keep kosher and steaks for anyone else who wants them."

"That's brilliant," Joy said. "We had our reception at the shul, and a chef who is one of our members did the cooking." She looked down at her blue skirt. "I'm going to change out of this dress. Meet you in the dining room in a few minutes."

Hillie picked up her tote bag and purse, scanning the room for anything she might have forgotten. She left her things near the front door and returned to the table as Joy reappeared in her yoga pants.

"More coffee?" Joy asked.

"I'm good, thanks. By the way, that was the best cup of tea I've ever had in my life."

Joy's expression brightened. "My own formulation. I have a blending room upstairs. You didn't see it, but there's a walk-in closet up there where I keep my teas and essential oils. I'm working on a line of tea to bring to market at some point." She patted her tummy. "If I can get past baby making, that is."

"Why am I just finding this out now?" Hillie said. "Your own line? That's so exciting!"

"It's been my dream since I worked as a tea barista in high school." Suddenly, she grew serious. "There is something else I'd like to talk to you about while you're here," she said. "Tamara's singing." She winced, and her mouth quirked to the side.

Hillie burst out laughing. Two seconds later, Joy collapsed into giggles that grew until her face turned red.

"What are we going to do?" Hillie said, when she could speak.

Sinking back into her chair in a dramatic move, Joy wiped tears from her face. "I have no idea."

"We don't want to hurt her feelings," Hillie said. "Never in a million years would we hurt her feelings."

"You're on your own, sister," Joy said, shaking her head. "Whatever you decide, I'm behind you 100%." She finished her glass of water, then stood up to find a key in a kitchen drawer. "Do you have time to take a quick tour of my blending room? We keep it locked, so the girls don't wander in."

Two hours later, they hugged good-bye and Hillie drove south. Entering the freeway, she commanded, "Call Jay," and her car dialed his number. In seconds his voice came over her car speakers.

She told him about her wonderful visit with Joy. "We have to get together with her and Reub more often."

"Absolutely. I'd love it!"

"I'll stop at the house on my way past," she said. "Will you be there?"

"I should be home around 7:00. I'll text you if it's going to be later."

"Okay. I'm thinking smothered chicken for dinner." She ended the call, happy they would spend the evening together. This had been a delightful day, and she wanted to share the rest of it with him.

The house felt like home when she stepped inside. She had stopped at the grocery for a few items and paused in the kitchen to put everything away. When she reached the bedroom to put down her tote bag, she froze. At the end of the bed, the wall was a candy-apple red color—beaming out like Rudolph's nose. How could she ever sleep in here? She had wanted this room white for a reason. She had told Jay that.

She went ahead with her plans for a home-cooked dinner, but the longer she thought about the bedroom, the angrier she grew. By the time Jay got home, she was laying for him. He sailed in with his usual hello kiss, but she turned her face aside. He drew up, instantly alert.

"What on earth made you think a red wall in the bedroom was okay?" she demanded.

His eyes narrowed. "We had all that leftover paint from the powder room," he said. "I thought red would be romantic. I wanted to surprise you."

"What color was my apartment?" she asked.

He took half a step back. "White."

"I need a blank room to be able to rest. We put red in the powder room because you're only there for under five minutes. No one is going to sleep in there."

"I'm sorry, babe." He looked dejected. "I thought I was doing something good."

She softened. "Just a two minute phone call, Jay. We've been through this before. All I'm asking is that you check in with me, and we make these decisions as a team."

"I'm so sorry. It was supposed to be a surprise. I thought you would be happy."

"Buy me a red nightie if you want romantic," she said. "Just don't make me look at a red wall when I'm trying to sleep."

"Getting white to cover that red is going to be a nightmare."

"Have you ever heard of primer?" she retorted. In a sad voice, she said, "Let's eat. I need to get home."

"You're not staying tonight?"

"This kind of thing makes me feel heartsick."

His eyebrows drew together. "What are you saying, Hillie?"

"Let's take Rabbi Sam up on his offer of continuing counseling after the wedding. When we run up on something like this, it will be easier if we have someone to give us both perspective. Don't you think?"

"That's not a problem. I like Rabbi Sam. He has common sense. That's hard to find these days."

"Done." She slid into his arms. "I'm tired of arguing. Let's make up."

He tightened his hold on her. "Now you're talking."

Chapter 14

The Final Weeks

Hillie: "Mom, how will I know I've found
the right man to marry?"

Hillie's Mother: "Find the man who will cherish you
for the rest of his life."

April passed as a steady stream of bridal showers and fittings, selecting music for the various playlists, along with finalizing the elements of the ceremony with Rabbi Sam.

May started the round of food tastings and cake tastings—each with cost comparisons and final decisions—and many trips to Temecula. Then selecting the gifts—gifts for the wedding party, for the guest book attendant, the vocal artist, favors for the guests, and on and on.

Searching through Etsy, Hillie found the perfect bridal-party gifts: monogrammed wine glasses with each name in beautiful script and underneath *Hilary and Jacob* and their wedding date. Guest favors would be stemless wine glasses with only *Hilary and Jacob* and the date. The stemless glasses would go on the tables, and everyone would take theirs home as a memento.

Hillie put in the orders and set the shipping address for Gershon Bachus.

Done.

Somewhere during the preparation frenzy, Jay got a bright idea—a Mother's Day surprise for Olivia. He and Hillie were driving back from Temecula on a Saturday afternoon when he told Hillie what he had in mind.

She stared. "A puppy?"

He looked so pleased with himself that Hillie burst out laughing. "What gave you that idea?" she asked.

"Think about it. She needs something to occupy her attention as well as keep her company. She has her charities and her work at the shul, but she's home alone with all that time to obsess over the wedding. Dad is still on the road four days a week and will be for several more years."

"Jock Jaworski," she declared, still watching him, "You are brilliant."

He looked like he was six years old with an A on his report card. "I've got it cleared with Dad, so I've been looking around to see what I can find."

"A Shih Tzu," Hillie said, nodding. "They are so loving and so darn cute."

"We need one that's six to eight weeks old, just ready to leave its mother. I read that puppies imprint to their owners when they come into the home very young."

Hillie called for Chinese takeout to pick up before they reached her apartment. When they arrived, they immediately went online to look for a Shih Tzu puppy. Mother's day was ten days away. They made a couple of calls and had a list to check out the following day.

The next morning after a late breakfast, they were back in the car. "What are we going to do if we find a puppy today?" Hillie asked. "Where will it stay until time Mother's Day? Both our leases say No Pets."

"Maybe they'll hold it for us," he said, unruffled. "If not, I'll get Ron to keep it for us. He's in his mother's garage. She's not going to kick him out."

By that evening, Ron was the proud sitter for a squirming, face-licking bundle of fur with liquid eyes and a black button nose on its baby face. The puppy had brown markings with a circle of white over his forehead.

When Jay and Hillie arrived at the Jaworski home on Mother's Day, Max had the doggie accessories hidden in the trunk of his car. Hillie held the puppy—yet unnamed—when Max let them in.

Hurried whispers at the door, then Olivia appeared. When she saw the puppy, her mouth came open. She looked from the dog to Max and Jay.

"Happy Mother's Day," Jay said. Hillie held the puppy out to Olivia.

The moment Olivia took that little guy into her arms, he was licking her face and wriggling with delight. She cooed over him and carried him into the living room. Instant adoration.

The three conspirators stayed in the hall, reveling in their success.

"Max?" Olivia called. "Come here and look at him. He's so cute!"

On June 1, Hillie drove to Gershon Bachus Vintners for her final appointment with Christina before the wedding. Her car was in the shop for service, so Jay had loaned her his beloved boring Mercedes. Their original plan had been for Jay to come along, but he got called into surgery at the last minute. He would join Hillie via Skype if she needed his input on anything.

This meeting was what Christina termed the Final Meeting. Everything for the wedding would be put in place today—for better or worse, for richer or poorer.

While they sat together at a table in the empty tasting room, Christina put the phone on speaker and called every vendor on the list—caterer, photographer, bakery, valet parking, the band—verifying their instructions and confirming that everything was correct and on schedule down to the last item on each list.

They examined the custom-labeled bottles of kosher-style wine. Hillie set one aside to take home, so Jay could see it and taste it. They had chosen the Blanco Mélange, a blend of Chardonnay, Pinot Gris and Viognier. Rabbi Sam suggested a white wine because red wine stains would be costly, especially to Hillie's dress.

"Here are the disposables for serving the food," Christina said, indicating stacks of elegant-looking plates in various sizes. The cutlery could have passed for real silver.

"These are all plastic?" Hillie asked, picking up a spoon. "They don't look it."

"They are worth every cent," Christina said. "I have the receipts here. I ordered enough for two hundred to allow for accidents." She handed Hillie the paperwork to add to her bulging file. "Rabbi Sam called me first thing this morning. He asked me to keep Olivia occupied as best I can while she's here. Do you have any ideas to help me out?"

"I've been thinking about that. My father is dating a lovely Jewish woman. The wedding might be a good way for them to get acquainted. Her name is Dot, and she's primed to help us with Olivia."

"We'll surround Olivia with love and hope for the best," Christina said. "That's all we can do." She shuffled papers. "Now for the music…"

They talked for another hour. Hillie's mind was on overload. Finally, she headed home after 4:00. Once she reached the 91, traffic crept along bumper to bumper and completely stopped for five minutes at a time.

Finally, an opening sprang up ahead. Traffic surged as one body. The Mercedes was doing forty-five miles an hour when Hillie rounded a curve to see traffic at a dead stop three hundred feet ahead. Hillie stood on the brake pedal, but it was no use. She smashed into the car ahead of her and immediately felt the jolt of someone else ramming into her from behind.

First her forehead slammed into the steering wheel, then her head flew back. She felt a pain in her left knee. Everything went black.

Jay's last office appointment of the day was ending when his private cellphone rang. It had a restricted number. "Yes?"

A deep stern voice said, "Jacob Jaworski?"

Jay's heart skipped a beat. "Yes. This is Dr. Jaworski."

"I'm Lieutenant Michael Bowen with the California State Police. A car registered under your name was in an accident on the 91 this afternoon."

"What? Is my fiancée okay?"

"She was semi-conscious when she left the scene of the accident, but I don't have any information on her status. She's been taken to Anaheim Regional Medical Center. Your car…"

"Forget the car…" He ended the call and picked up his work cellphone. He had hospital privileges at Anaheim—not that he was there often—and the hospital number was in his phone. His mouth was so dry he could hardly breathe.

His staff nurse paused at the open door, watching him closely. He held up his finger, signaling her to wait. While the number dialed he said, "Tell Dr. Taub I need to see him stat."

The hospital switchboard picked up, and Jay had the information he needed in less than a minute. In less than five minutes, he was backing Brian Taub's car out of its parking space. He still wore his white coat with his stethoscope draped around his neck.

"Don't get in an accident. Don't get in an accident," he chanted on the drive to the hospital. With no information, his imagination ran wild. He had to get to Hillie.

He burst through the doors of the ER. The smell of antiseptic enveloped him, and immediately he was in his element. Hillie looked up when he dashed into her room. She had an IV drip. A white-haired nurse was taking her blood pressure.

He grabbed Hillie's hand and scanned her face. She had a red bump on her forehead and the beginning of two black eyes. "I got here as fast as I could," he said. "Are you okay, honey?"

She squinted, dazed. "Jay. Your car…" she murmured.

"As long as you're okay," he said, leaning close to her, "that's all I care about." She had sparkles of glass in her hair.

"My head…" She touched the bump on her forehead.

Jay had his light out of his pocket to look into her eyes. They reacted normally.

The nurse spoke up. "We've got her scheduled for CT as soon as the room opens up. Her vitals are good, no signs of internal bleeding."

"My knee," Hillie said, wincing. "It hurts."

He pulled back the sheet to see bruising on her left knee.

"Already X-rayed," the nurse said. "It's bruised, not broken."

Jay introduced himself and asked about Hillie's medication. Soon afterward, the nurse went out.

"Call my dad," Hillie said. Her eyes drifted closed. Jay pulled a chair close to her bed and pulled out his phone.

By the time Larry and Dot arrived, they had the test results. Hillie had a concussion. She would stay under observation in the hospital overnight, then they would see about next steps.

While they waited for the hospital staff to get Hillie settled into her room, Dot went out to get them all some dinner. Jay had no plans to leave the hospital that night.

By the time daylight shone into her room the next morning, Hillie was moving slowly. She went into the bathroom and came out a few minutes later, sobbing.

Jay rushed to her. "Are you in pain?"

"My face! Look at my face. Our wedding pictures will be ruined."

"Oh, honey." He pulled her into a hug. "We still have two weeks. By that time whatever bruising might be left—if anything—will be fixed with makeup." He urged her toward the bed. "Get some rest. It's going to be fine. I promise."

She melted into her pillow, tears still streaming. "I feel like such a baby."

"Sleep, sweetheart," he said. "Don't worry about a thing. I'm right here. Sleep."

On morning rounds, Dr. Nagori appeared before breakfast. A young woman of Indian descent, she carried Hillie's metal file. Word had gotten out that Jay was a doctor. She shook Jay's hand and flipped open the file for him to take a look. "She's doing great," the doctor said. "I think she's good to go."

Jay scanned the chart and nodded. He let out the breath he had been holding for the past fifteen hours.

Dr. Nagori moved to the bed to check Hillie's eyes with a light. She spoke to Hillie. "Keep quiet. Lots of sleep. No stress."

Hillie said, "We're getting married in two weeks. No stress?"

"We'll work it out," Jay said, stepping to the other side of the bed. "Dot offered to help, and I'm sure the girls will help you, too."

They decided Hillie should stay at the rental house instead of walking the three flights to her apartment, at least for a few days.

She had taken three weeks' vacation for the wedding, so Hillie only used four sick days before her vacation began. Except for lingering pain in her knee and bearing a strong resemblance to a raccoon, she felt well enough to return to her own place the following weekend. She was supposed to be moving that week, but her energy had disappeared. She would work for thirty minutes, and then she had to lie down.

Jay had gone into overdrive with taking care of his totaled car, dealing with insurance companies, and worrying about Hillie. He got a rental car until he could find time to shop for a new vehicle. "After the honeymoon, I'll take care of it," he declared. "I don't have time to think about a new car right now."

Dot and Margo stepped in to help with any remaining wedding details, and—most importantly—to help Hillie move out of her apartment. She had to be completely out before the wedding because the honeymoon would last until the end of the month.

Dad and Dot took off three days, plus the weekend. Margo and Joy came over on Sunday. They teased and laughed and filled the apartment with love. Lying on her sofa, watching them together, Hillie's heart filled up with warmth. This was family.

Ten days after the accident, Hillie was still finding glass in her hair. The bruising around her eyes had faded to faint yellow that disappeared under a coating of concealer. Her knee still gave her a twinge now and then, but she was no longer in constant pain and could manage the steps to her apartment.

Two days before the Big Day, Hillie settled into the Garden Suite at The Hotel Temecula in Old Town, just minutes from Gershon Bachus. The next time she saw Jay, they would be at the rehearsal.

Hillie's early arrival in Temecula was Jay's idea, and it was a great one. Surrounding herself with history made her happy. After their first date at Avila Adobe, The Hotel Temecula felt like circling back to the beginning of their love story.

The hotel had its original 1800s furniture, along with artifacts and a sign in her room announcing the hotel had installed the new Edison Lights with a warning about not lighting them with a match.

The day before the wedding, Amanda took care of the bridesmaids during their spa day while Hillie pampered herself with a mani-pedi and facial right there in her hotel room.

Dad and Dot booked a room at the same hotel and drove her to the rehearsal that evening.

"I can drive," she had said, when Larry suggested they drive her.

"Let me pamper you," he said, pulling her into a soft hug. "It's my last day to have you as my single daughter."

Her arms tightened around him. "I love you, Daddy."

When Hillie arrived at Gershon Bachus Vintners, Rabbi Sam and Christina had everything prepared for the rehearsal. The walk-through began smoothly. Cloe and Zoe stayed at about half their normal speed, and they did just fine.

Tamara started her song, stopped, tried again, and burst into tears. "I can't get the timing right," she said. "I'm so sorry, Jay. I can't get it right."

Jay hurried to comfort her. Hillie watched them, sending up a prayer for help.

Christina brought some wireless ear buds to Tamara. "Here, put these in. The soundtrack has two options, one with someone singing the words and one with just the music. Put these in, and I'll play the track with the singer so you can follow her." She smiled at Tamara. "Will that work?"

Rabbi Sam said, "It's a lot of pressure, Tamara, but you're going to do just fine. Thank you, Christina. That's a brilliant idea."

Tamara nodded. "I'll practice it that way," she said, returning to the bridesmaid line.

Twenty minutes later, they all headed for their cars and the rehearsal dinner.

That night, Hillie stepped into her hotel room to find a dozen red roses waiting for her. The card said, "Sleep well, my love. Tomorrow is ours. Jay."

Chapter 15

The Big Day

The recipe for a successful marriage:
The 5 L's: Love, Listen, Learn, Live and Laugh
~ **Rabbi Marc Rubenstein**

At 10:00 the next morning, Hillie arrived at Gershon Bachus wearing sweats and a polo shirt, her hair still damp from the shower. The bridesmaids and two hairdressers were already in the Bridal Room. Amanda and Sally were in the first stages of their up-dos. Tamara had ear buds in, eyes closed, softly singing in a corner.

Near the back of the room, Cara was in whispered conversation with Joy and Becca. They looked up when Hillie came in. Cara was in tears.

"What's going on?" Hillie asked, dropping her bags near the door.

Joy spoke up. "Cara forgot her dress. She thought it was in her stuff, but it's not."

Immediately, Hillie went into solution mode. She pulled out her phone. No signal. She forgot the winery didn't get cell service. Looking around, she spotted a house phone, got an outside line, and dialed the number from her phone contacts. As it rang she said, "Is the dress at your place, Cara?"

The distraught girl nodded.

Hillie spoke into the receiver. "Hi Margo. It's Hillie. Are you still at home?" She paused for the answer, then she told Margo the situation and handed the phone to Cara. "Give her your address, then call someone to give her access to your apartment."

While Cara talked, Joy gave Hillie a high five. "Great save!"

"You look adorable," Hillie said, looking over Joy's blue dress.

She modeled it, turning side to side. "I put it on to show the girls," Joy said. "You are right. Raquel is an angel."

Shortly afterward, Dot arrived carrying a wide box loaded with breakfast sandwiches and other goodies. She came near Hillie and pointed out the chaise near the French doors. "Hillie, your job today is to stretch out there. Relax and look pretty. Please tell me if you need anything at all. That's what I'm here for."

Hillie hugged her. "Thank you, Dot. Thank you so much."

"My pleasure," the older woman said, returning the hug. She looked around and focused on the ironing station nearby. "In the meantime, I'll get the ironing board cranked up and ready."

Hillie kicked off her shoes and stretched out. Joy brought her a sandwich and coffee.

The female photographer arrived and starting snapping photos of the various stages of preparation.

Shortly after noon, Brian Taub came to the door and handed in a large rectangular package—Jay's gift for Hillie, along with a handwritten note. Hillie was in the hairdresser's chair. All the bridesmaids would have their hair up, but Hillie's dark curls would stay down.

"Do you have anything for Jay?" Amanda asked, her body blocking the partly open door from the view of the man outside.

Hillie got up to find her note for Jay in her tote bag. "I'll give him my gift myself after the ceremony. I want to see his face when he opens it." Handing the note to Amanda, she tore the wrapping from her package. It was a mirror surround by ornamental gold. A little plaque on the bottom said,

> *Hillie,*
> *When you look into this mirror,*
> *always remember you are seeing*
> *the woman I love.*
> *Jay*

A round of *Awww*'s went through the room. The photographer went into action.

Before Hillie knew it, makeup was done, shoes were on, and all the girls lined up on the landing for some pre-ceremony photos right before Christina started the procession music. The lady photographer stayed to take pictures of Hillie with her dad while the male photographer worked outside.

When Larry stepped into the Bridal Room and caught sight of Hillie, he froze, his stunned expression turning to wonder.

She stood in a pool of light from a nearby window. Her creamy shoulders made an exquisite background for her moonstone necklace. The gown glided down her slim form, hugging her all the way to the floor with a small train behind her.

The dress was a gift from her mother. The Mantilla style veil was all Hillie. It took her back to her First Communion. Scalloped lace draped over her forehead and down both her cheeks, down her front to swoop back into a cathedral style that reached beyond her dress to trail behind her. Filmy white organza embraced her. She felt like an angel.

Larry stood close to her, his eyes glistening. "If your mother could see you now," he murmured.

"She can, Daddy," Hillie said. "I know she can." She blinked.

"Jay's a fine man," he said, smiling gently. "You did good. She would approve."

Hillie reached up to kiss his cheek.

Larry handed her the bride's bouquet of white roses and blue hydrangeas and offered her his arm. Covering her hand with his, he said, "Let's take those stairs nice and slow."

They paused inside the double doors with one barely open to listen until the music sounded for the bride's entrance. Rustling sounds told them the guests were standing.

When they stepped out to the landing, for a few seconds they had a panoramic view of the wedding from above—the white Chuppah under the gazebo, the table near the back with the gilt-framed Ketubah on a stand, Rabbi Sam looking distinguished in a blue suit with a white yarmulke and tallit. The girls in their pearls with up-dos and dangly earrings, the guys in navy suits and blue ties—and the twins wearing matching white dresses with white baskets for the rose petals that now covered the silk runner.

Slightly to the right of the bridesmaids, a small lace-covered table displayed a picture of Hillie's mother in a silver frame with a low white candle flickering in front of it, the wedding album nearby.

Moving in slow motion, Hillie took each step with care, gazing at all the smiling faces as she passed. Near the front, Olivia held her puppy. He had on a little black tux with a little black tie.

When Hillie met Jay's gaze, everything else vanished. He wore a white tux with a white bow tie and white yarmulke. He tried to smile at her through his tears, and she realized that her own face was wet. Dot furtively handed Hillie a tissue while she and Larry paused in the aisle.

Rabbi Sam said, "Who gives this woman to be with this man?"

Larry said, "Her mother and I." He kissed Hillie and hugged her close for a long moment.

From her peripheral vision Hillie saw Reuben's mother at the side aisle, taking the twins out as planned. She would treat them to ice cream and fun, then see them safely home.

When Larry reached his seat, Rabbi Sam said, "Good evening and welcome to this most important moment for Hillie and Jay. Today is a celebration of love, of commitment, of family, and of two people who are making promises to each other forever."

He glanced from Hillie to Jay, "As I see tears in your eyes, it is my wish for you that you always cry in each other's tears and laugh in each other's smiles."

He turned to Max and Olivia. "Hillie and Jay are an exemplary couple, so we'd like to take this moment to honor their parents—Max and Olivia Jaworski… and Larry and Melissa Gordon—for the magnificent job you did in raising these fine young people."

Indicating the lace-covered table, he said, "We have set this table here with these mementos of Hillie's mother, Melissa Gordon, who has been a vibrant part of this whole process, though she is no longer with us. The dress Hillie wears today is her mother's wedding gown. If you always love the one you lose, you will never lose the one you love."

He reached behind him to lift two orchids and handed one to Hillie and one to Jay. Jay gave his to Olivia and hugged her. Hillie lay the orchid in front of her mother's picture, then hugged her dad.

Rabbi Sam continued, "We'd like to take a moment to honor others we love who have passed on but remain in our hearts—Jay's grandparents, Herb and Midge Greenburg, his Uncle Jordy Jaworski and his aunt Guta Daily."

Olivia nodded and dabbed her eyes with a tissue. Max took the puppy onto his lap.

Rabbi Sam stepped into position under the Chuppah. Hillie and Jay followed him and faced each other, holding hands. Rabbi Sam said, "As you give each other your hand to hold, may you give each other your heart to keep."

He went on, "The Chuppah is a simple shelter, which represents the promise of the home Hillie and Jay will create together. Hillie is an interior designer, so their home will be beautiful. The four pillars of the Chuppah represent the four pillars upon which a strong home is built: family, friendship, love and respect.

"A shelter that is open on all four sides symbolizes the importance of community and of participation in each other's lives. Hillie and Jay, may your home be filled with the joy of family and friends, a shelter against the storms, a haven of peace, a stronghold of faith and love."

He poured wine into a gold encrusted glass. "I'd like everyone here to think of a wish for this sacred marriage. And," nodding to Hillie and Jay, "I'd also like you to think of a wish for your marriage before you drink from this cup. And may your wishes be fulfilled."

He lifted the glass. "Think of that wish as we say the Jewish blessing." He spoke the blessing in Hebrew, then English, and handed the glass to Jay, who sipped and shared it with Hillie.

Members of the bridal party stepped to a microphone to the left of the gazebo to read the Seven Blessings.

When they finished, Rabbi Sam said, "I'd like everyone to think of a memory that you have of Hillie and Jay, separately and together, while I tell a little about their story.

"Hillie and Jay met four years ago on a blind date. They were introduced by dear friends who are here today." He told the story of their visit to Avila Adobe and Jay's proposal as their hot air balloon passed over this very spot. "I have seen their love for each other in the way they play together and laugh together, and also how they are quick to resolve their differences and work as a team."

He said a blessing in Hebrew followed by the English translation, then nodded to Jay.

Noticeably trembling, Jay pulled a page from his pocket and opened it. "Hillie, you are the most beautiful woman I've ever seen—inside and out. I love your spirit. You see an opportunity, and you rush out to meet it. I know I can depend on you because you always keep your word. When I'm down, you find a way to make me smile and lift me up. You have wisdom that goes straight to the heart of an issue but without blame or negativity. And best of all, you don't take things too seriously. You know how to laugh at life, at yourself, and especially at me." He grinned at her and chuckles went through the audience. "You make me a better man."

Hillie drew in a breath to collect herself. "Jay, your kind spirit captured my heart from the first time I met you. You have the strength of a royal palm tree with deep roots that weathers the storm as it bends and sways with the wind. You work hard, but you also know how to play. You are wise and understanding, faithful and true. You gave me the confidence to place my hand in yours now and forever."

Introductory music came over the loudspeaker. Tamara touched her ear buds and moved to the microphone. She closed her eyes to concentrate.

The voice of the vocalist from the soundtrack came over the loudspeakers. Startled, Hillie looked first at Tamara singing into a dead microphone, then at Christina blithely smiling near the sound system controls. Jay gave Hillie's hand the barest tug. Like a partner in crime, he gave her a silent signal, *Play it cool.*

She swallowed back a giggle and forced her face to remain passive.

At the end of the song, polite applause and Tamara returned to her place in the line of bridesmaids. Rabbi Sam nodded to Jay to begin the vows.

Jay looked into her eyes. "Hillie, you are the light of my life. Over the past couple of weeks, that has become more real to me than ever. You are breath to me because when I thought you were hurt, I couldn't breathe." He paused, filled with emotion.

In a quavering voice he went on, "I want you to know that you can always count on me. I promise to take you to my heart as you are and as you will be. I will be your sanctuary. I will be your warmth with my full loyalty and trust. With my whole heart, body, and soul, and with these hands of mine," he showed her his hands, tears streaming now, "I will cherish, protect, and honor you as long as we both shall live."

Hillie lifted his hand to her lips.

"Jay, I accept your promise and give to you my promise that I will be your faithful companion, your lover and your friend. I will be strength. I will be light, and I will be hope."

With a catch in her voice, she said, "I want you to always feel like your dreams have come true when you are with me, that nothing is impossible, and we will build an amazing future together. I will love you every day… as if it were our first and as if it were our last, as if there were no tomorrow, forever yours from this day forward as long as we both shall live."

Rabbi Sam led them through the *I Do's* and asked for the rings. Brian handed him a small velvet box.

"The next rite is the symbolism of the rings. A wiser man, wiser than myself, King Solomon said that a wife and a husband should wear a token of their love on their finger to show you have taken a vow holy unto G-d." He handed a ring to Jay. "Jay place this ring on Hillie's finger, look into her eyes, the gateway to her soul, and repeat after me, 'I am my beloved's and she is all mine!'"

Jay spoke the words. Hillie did the same. She felt the smooth band with her thumb as Rabbi Sam brought out another glass of wine and gave another blessing.

He gestured toward the Ketubah on the table. "Another element we observe is the Ketubah that we are going to sign after the ceremony is over. In the Ketubah, Jay promises Hillie three things: that there will be food on the table and a roof over her head and that he will always have love for her in his heart."

He lifted the two ends of the tallit and touched each of their shoulders. "I'd like to give you the priestly blessing, the blessing of Aaron. May G-d bless you and keep you. May G-d's countenance be upon you and be gracious unto you, and may you have *Mazel Tov!* all the days of your life." He let the tallit fall back into place. "As we all say, Amen." He turned to the table behind him for a moment.

When he returned, he held a white cloth bundle in his hands. "It is a custom to end the ceremony with the breaking of the glass. In the Jewish faith, it is customary to say *Mazel Tov!* when the glass is broken, which means Good Luck to the couple."

He went on, "The fragility of the glass reminds us that love, like glass, is fragile and must be protected. A broken glass cannot be fully mended. Likewise the promises you made today are irreversible. Just as this glass is broken into so many pieces it's impossible to count them, so, too, are our innumerable wishes for a lifetime of good health, prosperity, success, and happiness together."

He placed the bundle on the gazebo floor. Jay stamped it with a loud POP.

"*Mazel Tov!*" from the crowd.

"By the power vested in me, as witnessed by friends and family, I now pronounce you husband and wife. You may kiss your wife."

Jay pulled Hillie close and kissed her.

"For the first time since the creation of the world, I present to you Mr. and Mrs. Jacob Jaworski."

Lively music, laughter and applause—Jay and Hillie headed down the aisle and straight up the stairs. They reached the Bridal Room laughing and exhilarated.

"It was perfect!" Jay said. He pulled her to him for a kiss. "You are so beautiful, Hillie. You took my breath away."

They spend the next few minutes reveling in each other.

Finally Hillie asked, "Was that a mistake with Tamara's song? Christina played the voice track over the speakers."

Jay chuckled. "Whether it was a mistake or not, it was fabulous. Tamara didn't have a clue."

Hillie laughed. "I should send Christina a bonus for that one!" She glanced at a silver gift bag on the table. "Oh, I have something for you. In the excitement, I almost forgot." She handed him the bag. "Here, open this."

She giggled, watching him pull out a wad of crumpled tissue paper. "Careful," she said. "It's breakable."

He glanced at her and unwrapped a wine glass. It was engraved with the acronym G.L.A.S.S. and underneath, Groom Likes a Simple

Service. Jay chuckled. He turned it in the light for a better view. "How did you think of that?"

"One of my brighter moments." Carefully pulling her veil forward, she perched on the chaise. "We have to go out for pictures soon. I'd best rest a few minutes."

"How are you?" he asked, instantly concerned. "How's your head?"

"It's okay," she said. "Surprisingly well, actually."

He brought her a bottle of water and sat beside her. Reaching into his inside coat pocket, he pulled out a long envelope. "I hope you packed for the beach," he said, handing it to her.

"What?" She looked at him as she opened the envelope and unfolded the page. "Jay!" she cried, then tilted her head back, laughing for sheer joy. "Rancho Las Cruces! For our honeymoon?" She threw her arms around him.

He held her close. "Two whole weeks in heaven, Hillie."

She turned her face toward him for another kiss. "I'm already there."

About the Author

An interfaith pioneer, Rabbi Marc Rubenstein is a distinguished Hebrew scholar. He studied at the Hebrew University in Jerusalem before obtaining his B.A. in Religion and History Studies at American University in Washington,  D.C. He received his rabbinical training at the Academy for Jewish Religion in New York City and also studied at New York University and Ohio State University.

President or Vice President of the East Bay Council of Rabbis in the San Francisco Bay Area for more than two years, he was also Rabbi at Temple Isaiah in Newport Beach for more than twenty years. Rabbi Marc is licensed to perform weddings in twenty-two states and also served as the official rabbi for Disneyland. He works with and is a member of Great Officiants in Southern California.

Rabbi Marc considers himself a mentor for life and continues working with his wedding couples throughout their lifecycle events. He has officiated at life events for many celebrities and dignitaries. Once he performed a wedding in Jay Leno's garage.

An inspiration to thousands of unaffiliated and independent Jews and interfaith families, he is a contributing writer for local outlets and *The Jewish Journal*. He counsels people who are children of

Holocaust survivors and people who are grieving. An acclaimed teacher and public speaker, he is a favorite of Hebrew School students as well as Bar Mitzvah and Bat Mitzvah candidates. He is the author of the Jewish children's book, *The Kingdom of Onion*.

Rabbi Marc lives with his wife Margery in Temecula, California.

50 Things Rabbi Marc Rubenstein Does at a Wedding Service That Other Rabbis Might Not Do

1. At beginning of the ceremony: Meet and greet the wedding guests and ask everyone to think of a memory they have of the wedding couple, both separately and together. They think of it looking at the couple who are standing at the altar. This brings all friends and all families into the wedding.
2. Mention those who are not present at the wedding ceremony, those who have passed on, and those who are there in spirit but not in body to honor their memory: "If we always love the one we lose, we never lose the one we love."
3. Have all the guests think of a special wish for the wedding couple, when I bless the first glass of wine. Think of the wish and wish the wish into the glass of wine. This brings friends and the family into the wedding service.
4. Tell a story of the wedding couple rather than a wedding homily.
5. Personalized wedding vows.
6. Giving of roses or orchid to the mothers as a sign of honoring them for bringing up their son or daughter for the person that they grew up to be. Last thing that they do as a single adult and the first thing that they do as a married couple.

7. Hand over the heart ceremony.

8. My wish for the wedding couple. "As I give you my hand to hold, I give you my heart to keep. May you cry in each other's tears and laugh in each other's smile." This is done when they place the ring on each other's fingers.

9. Reading of "No man without a woman, no woman without a man, and neither without G-d." (Verse from King Solomon)

10. "Hand over hands" ceremony and reading.

11. Using white wine instead of red wine in case the wine spills.

12. Use of a light bulb for the Breaking of the Glass: It makes better POP.

13. Special explanation of the priestly benediction as I wrap the prayer shawl around the wedding couple.

14. Pronouncement: To the bride and groom. "And since the first time of the creation of the world here in (wherever the city is) as husband and wife."

15. Moving out of the way when bride and groom kiss as I stand aside so that I am not captured in the photograph or a part of their wedding kiss.

16. Matching my wedding attire to the colors of the wedding.

17. Meet with the couple an unlimited number of meetings to get to know them and discuss their wedding.

18. Attending the wedding rehearsal.

19. Arriving one hour before the wedding to make sure things are just right.

20. Providing a choice of Ketubah for the wedding couple as my wedding gift to them.

21. Provide a frame for the wedding Ketubah as a wedding gift to the couple

22. Providing a beautiful birch Chuppah for the wedding couple at no charge.

23. Officiating only one wedding per day. Most rabbis rush weddings to get to their next one, especially if the wedding runs late, since it almost always does.

24. Traveling to meet the couple rather than have couple travel to meet the rabbi at his office.

25. Wedding pre-counseling with unlimited counseling meetings with the wedding couple.

26. Officiating at interfaith weddings with other religious non-Jewish clergy. Celebrating and taking the religion to the couple rather than taking the couple and putting it into the religion. This avoids the Cookie-cutter Wedding Syndrome.

27. Adding personalized humor and romance verses and sentences into the half-hour ceremony, creating spirituality, putting it into the wedding and adding to the religious traditional symbols of the Jewish interfaith wedding. Most of my wedding ceremonies last 22 ½ minutes. Example: "If we were to add up the frequent flyers miles that were accumulated here today, it would not equal the amount of love the couple has for you and each other in their hearts."

28. Adding the four elements of nature into the wedding. The earth we stand on. The water of the ocean. The spirit or wind of G-d and the Angels. And the fire or the passion that is only the couple's hearts.

29. Never been late for anyone's wedding.

30. Always Prepared.

31. Check the microphones at most weddings. At many weddings, people cannot hear the bride and groom's vows.

32. Get my hair professionally done for each wedding.

33. Never bother the wedding couple if something goes wrong at the wedding and always work with the venue and the wedding coordinator to fix the problem.

34. Making sure you keep your own personal record of officiating at the marriage and the wedding ceremony.

35. Making sure that the Chuppah is in place so it doesn't fall down.

36. Making sure that the ring bearer and flower girl go potty just before the wedding so the ceremony doesn't have to pause for a potty break.

37. Allowing the wedding coordinator, the photographer, the venue, and the bride and groom decide when the wedding actually begins. The rabbi isn't the decision maker here!

38. Meeting with other clergy if wedding is co-officiated before the ceremony at a separate meeting to plan the wedding ceremony.

39. Helping couple plan their own wedding website.

40. Putting personal humor into the service when appropriate.

41. Staying for a wedding picture with the couple.

42. Taking a rabbinical assistant to help prepare the table under the Chuppah and carry wedding items necessary for use in the ceremony.

43. No extra charge if wedding starts late.

44. No extra charge for gas or miles outside a certain driving radius.

45. Encouraging an ongoing relationship with the wedding couple for other lifecycle spiritual events throughout the marriage.

46. Free marital counseling after the wedding ceremony into the marriage, on an as-needed basis.

47. Providing tallit for priestly benediction and to decorate the Chuppah as well.

48. Providing yarmulkes for all the wedding guests.

49. Staying for at least the cocktail hour after the wedding.

50. Staying for the wedding meal, if invited.

Notes

Morgan James
Speakers Group

 www.TheMorganJamesSpeakersGroup.com

We connect Morgan James published
authors with live and online events
and audiences whom will benefit
from their expertise.

Morgan James makes all of our titles available
through the Library for All Charity Organization.

www.LibraryForAll.org

Printed in the USA
CPSIA information can be obtained
at www.ICGtesting.com
JSHW022332140824
68134JS00019B/1432